Queen
and Country

Finn Maedan

Names have been changed to protect the
identities of those still serving their country.

ISBN-13: 978-1484977989

ISBN-10: 148497798X

DEDICATION

For my beautiful wife and six wonderful children.

CONTENTS

PREFACE

Hanslope Park, in the heart of unspoilt Buckinghamshire, is home to Her Majesty's Government Communications Centre - HMGCC for short. Hanslope Park is much more than a centre of expertise. Over five hundred government scientists and technicians work here on a whole range of customer-driven projects. Research, design and development of unique communications systems, hardware and software specifically for HM Government - for use both at home and overseas.

It is also home to MI6's Technical Security Department (TSD), staffed by Secret Intelligence Service technical operatives who process and analyse data sent from GCHQ in Cheltenham and RAF Menwith Hill in North Yorkshire, especially data intercepted from the foreign embassies in London. Following WWII during the early Cold War era, this function was known as the Diplomatic Wireless Service.

Wikimapia.org 2012.

FOREWORD

If you're looking for an expose into the inner secrets of the Intelligence Services this isn't it. If you're looking for the twisting plot of a new Bond film this isn't it. My name is Finn Maedan and this is my story of 14 years working for the British Government in the then ultra-secretive Operational Security Department or OSD.

In the autumn of 1982 at the age of 17 and at the height of the Cold War I joined a training scheme at the Foreign & Commonwealth Office. Following two years in 'The Park' training school I spent the next 11 years travelling the world as a member of Operational Security Department. OSD in the 80's was a Government department based at The Park numbering around 200. At any one time 60 - 70% of its operatives would be overseas either on short trips or full posting. Short trips could be anything from a few days to three months and a full posting would be two to four years. The departments principle role was counter espionage, protecting Embassies and staff from electronic attack and ensuring secure facilities for the gathering and transmission of data.

Publicly, OSD was attached to the Foreign & Commonwealth Office and it worked primarily for MI6 and the FCO with the odd function here and there for MI5 and the MOD. As a consequence we had to fit into all worlds and at one point I had a Diplomatic grade (DS8), a military grade (Second Lieutenant) and a civil service grade (TTO) at the same time. Most of our work was in British Embassies, British High Commissions and British Consulates overseas but I also had 'jobs' in Army bases, foreign Embassies, NATO, Whitehall London, Cabinet Office London and our home base, The Park.

Three decades on with most secrets declassified and my memory fading rapidly, now is the time to pass on a few stories to whoever cares. Like most jobs, 90% of what we did was run of the mill, mundane even, and up until now I have never really shared much of what went on.

This is the other 10%...

PROLOGUE

Khartoum, Sudan 1985

The Ford Cortina's rear window was gone. A couple of AK 47 bullets had made sure of that and the spook curled up in the fetal position on the back seat was covered in small pieces of shattered glass. He was screaming at my boss D who had just driven us straight through a road block on the airport road in Khartoum, leaning out of his window and shouting 'We're fucking diplomats you pricks!'.

Following an afternoon 'goodbye Sudan' session, D was completely pissed and now laughing as he accelerated away from the boy soldiers who had just unloaded their rifle magazines in our direction. Fortunately for us the guns they had were old, some jammed, some misfiring and some too heavy for the young boy trying to lift it. The spook was just screaming 'you stupid fuck' over and over and I don't mind admitting I was shitting myself. The adrenalin was rushing and with the airport just ahead, a wave of relief started to take over when we spotted even more soldiers in front of us, this time standing in front of a tank. The almost laughable irony was that having been shot at trying to get there, the airport was now surrounded by military hardware and completely shut off to the public. A military coup had started hours earlier and the General was about to seize power.

I'm not sure if it was the adrenalin kicking in or the tank barrel pointed straight at us but D was a bit smarter this time and hit the brakes as the soldiers waved us down. There was no negotiating, it didn't matter who we were and normal rules did not apply. There was nothing we could do other than return to the embassy. It was two days before my 21st birthday and I sat in the passenger seat with my pissed boss muttering 'wankers' under his breath struggling to find 1st gear and an angry spook in the rear telling him his career was over. Not for the first time I was wondering how the fuck I ended up here.

ONE

The Park 1981
THE INTERVIEW

Shakin' Stevens was at No 1 in the charts with 'Green Door', raiders of the Lost Ark had just been released at the cinema and the MAZE IRA hunger strikes had just ended.

At 15 I had to move to Milton Keynes. It was non-negotiable as the whole family were following my dad's job which had been relocated to the area. I absolutely hated it. Up until then I had a thriving social life, a great set of mates, messed around at school and had absolutely no idea what I was going to do with my life – and I loved it. Suddenly I was in the fourth house to be built on a muddy building site in the middle of nowhere later to be called Newlands, one of the estates in the grand social experiment known as Milton

Keynes.

I was legally obliged to attend one more year of school and registered with the nearest one, Newland High. Newland was another experiment in that all teachers were addressed by their first name, there were break out areas for each year group (ours had a pool table), the Sixth form did not have to attend lessons unless they wanted to. There was even a student smoking room.

I didn't do much at Newland but needed to top up my abysmal total of 3 o 'levels by doing a few re-sits.

I remember one afternoon being called to Mervyns' office, my Head of Year, to discuss my future plans. He soon found out I wasn't interested in University and had no intention of doing A levels, all I wanted was to get out there and earn some money.

One of the few good things about MK at the time was its high employment rate due to more and more companies relocating there and as a consequence there was construction everywhere you looked. I was confident I would get a job but had no idea what I wanted to do. Mervyn told me about a few local training opportunities including amongst other things a Mechanical Engineering Apprenticeship scheme where the top 10% went on to work for Westland Helicopters. That seemed pretty cool at the time and not only would I end up with a certificate in

FINN MAEDAN

Mechanical Engineering but I would be paid while doing it. I was sold.

The engineering course was hard work but fun. We had to clock in and out with every minute missed docked automatically from your pay. Like any environment full of blokes there was lots of banter and a steady stream of practical jokes but ultimately safety was everything particularly when arc welding or using an industrial lathe. The training was divided into five sections; milling, turning, welding, Tec drawing and electrical. We would draw the item we were going to create before going through the various departments building and finishing it.

One lunchtime Mr. G the electrical instructor called me into his office. He asked me what my plans were when I'd finished the course. I told him I started it with the intention of getting into Westlands to which he replied;

'Maedan, I've got good news and bad news' in his heavy Glaswegian accent.

'If I'm honest you're probably not going to make the top 10 for Westlands.' I pretty much knew this but him confirming it was still a bummer.

'The good news is I have been asked to keep an eye out for a few lads that fit a specific criteria for a trainee position at The Park.' I had absolutely no idea what he was talking about.

13

'It's just an application form at this stage but I'm putting you forward if you fancy it.'

'Fine but a trainee what?'

'Worry about that if you make it to interview stage Maedan – for now just fill out the form.'

So I did.

About 3 months later I'd finished the engineering apprenticeship, passed and now had my CITB Mechanical Engineers Diploma. It was no shock that my name was missing when we heard the 10 Westland names called out but it didn't really matter to me as somehow I'd managed to blag my way into a local engineering company that manufactured test equipment.

At 17 I wasn't allowed to weld or use the lathes yet so I was pretty much a gofer for Big Mickey the Chief Lathe Operator , but at least I was a paid gofer. Big Mickey was a bear of a man with massive hands and a scar on his cheek that he said he got in Northern Ireland, but all the other blokes said he did working on his beloved Ford Capri when the bonnet dropped on him. Of course no one was going to say that to Big Mickey so instead we had to listen to his bullshit war stories most lunch breaks. Life there was pretty boring but I was doing OK and the fact that Big Mickey hadn't got rid of me meant I was doing something right. I was just waiting for my 18th birthday so I could get on the decent kit.

It was a total surprise then when one rainy Tuesday afternoon the company owner called me in to his office.

'Finn, you may be surprised to know, I actually quite like you'

'Thanks' I said puzzled.

'Michael tells me you are keen and a quick learner so it's with a little regret that I have to give you this.'

I was still laughing inside at the way he said Michael and was thinking about bringing that one up next lunch break when he handed me a letter. Bollocks, I thought to myself. Getting the boot and I was just beginning to enjoy it.

'Thanks' I said pathetically and got up to leave

'Where you going? Open it.'

I opened the letter.

It had a government crest at the top. Short and sweet it said;

Dear Mr Maedan

We are pleased to tell you that you have been selected for interview.

A vehicle will pick you up from your place of residence at 8am on Tuesday.

You will be returned that evening.

Yours

Head of Training.

It was signed with an unintelligible squiggle.

To this day I don't know why they didn't just send the letter to my address rather than deliver it through my existing boss but I guess they had their reasons, and to be fair he was nothing other than encouraging telling me what a fantastic opportunity it was. I still didn't even know what I had applied for.

The day of the interview I got up early, made a cup of tea and sat waiting for a car. The previous afternoon the boss had come down to the shop floor to see me and offer his last words of wisdom.

'Dress smart and don't fuck it up'

That was it. No tips, no 'good luck' just 'don't fuck it up.' Brilliant.

After he walked back up to his office A loud 'ooooooh' came from Big Mickey. His good luck token was to cover my head in Swarfega (An industrial hand cleaner otherwise known as green gunk) followed by 'You'll be perfect. The place is full of tossers.' Charming.

I had my smartest gear on. I didn't own a suit but had a pair of plain black trousers and a burgundy leather box jacket (please remember at this point it was 1981). I finished the look off with a skinny black tie and my fake gold tie collar pin that I'd bought from Wolerton Agora market just for the occasion.

Don't let anyone say I didn't make an effort!

The car that they had sent wasn't a car at all, it was a blue minibus and I must have been the last on the pickup run as there were already six other lads sitting there, none of whom I had ever seen before.

The first thing I noticed was that they were all wearing suits.

It was only about a 15 minutes from Newlands to The Park but no one spoke on the entire journey. I had never even heard of The Park at that point and it was quite a daunting sight pulling up to the high security gates. We were met by a couple of security guards, one of which boarded the minibus to ask for passports. No one told me that you had to take your passport along so I felt great having to get off the minibus while the six suited nerds held theirs out with big smiles on their faces. The security guard showed me into a waiting room and said he would make a phone call as there was no protocol for someone turning up with no ID. I was off to a great start.

Eventually I was met by a smartly dressed guy in his twenties and after a brief chat with the security guard, who he clearly knew, he told me we were going to walk to 'The House' where the interview day was taking place.

We walked past a large open garage that had a variety of vehicles in it from saloon cars to large trucks, all of which were painted the same blue with one exception which was a green Army fire engine.

The guy escorting me never did tell me his name but he said he had started as a trainee and remembered his interview day. He said try and relax and remember that however obscure the question you are asked, there is a reason they are asking it. Great, I thought – more riddles.

We finally got to the front door of 'The House' which turned out to be a large manor house acquired by the government after the war and now converted into offices. He paused before opening the door and said;

'In case it helps, remember The Times, Foreign Affairs and Richard Jenkins.' I thanked him but had absolutely no idea what he was talking about.

I was shown into a large wood paneled, windowless room that had a long table down the middle, board room style. Already sat smartly in place were the six smirking nerds from my minibus along with another six nerds who must have been picked up separately. I sat down at the only available seat and an elderly guy in a brown suit at the front of the room looked directly at me and said;

'Finally – we can start now.' Strike one against me I thought.

The door opened and a man in his forties wearing a grey suit walked in holding a tray covered in what looked like a tea-towel. I guessed straight away this was going to be a memory test so made sure I got a good look at the Tower of London design on the tea-towel. He placed the tray in the middle of the table. Brown suit nodded at grey suit and he removed the tea-towel. The tray was full of about 20 random objects from a pair of nutcrackers to what looked like a car air filter to me. Before I could take it all in, the tea-towel went back on. It felt like seconds that we had to view the items but we later found out it was 5 minutes. I used my exam memory method of making a sentence using the initial letters of the objects.

Brown suit circled the table like a huge vulture and placed a piece of paper and a pencil in front of all of us. He walked back to his position of control at the head of the boardroom table and said;

'You have 15 minutes.'

One of the geeks looked up completely puzzled and started trying to catch someone's attention as if he needed guidance. OK brown suit 1 hadn't told us what he wanted but if you hadn't worked it out by now you shouldn't be in the room.

I think I recalled at least 15 of the items and I added the fact it was a Tower of London design on the tea-towel but we were never told how we did.

After that test we were told there would be

three more tests that morning followed by a panel interview in the afternoon. The next two tests were Maths and English based psychometric examinations, the style of which I had seen before and were relatively straight forward. The cleverest test came next.

We had just been for a coffee break outside the room when we came back in for the final test of the morning. The smiling geeks were not so jolly now as the day was taking its mental toll. Brown suit walked back in and again placed lined pieces of paper in front of each of us as well as a pencil sharpened at both ends.

'Gentlemen, you will notice that in front of you I have placed three sheets of lined paper and a pencil sharpened at both ends. Why sharpened at both ends you may ask? Because today I am feeling generous and if one end breaks you have another chance. You have exactly 1 hour.' With that he left the room.

It was both hilarious and genius. Half the geeks were going into meltdown wandering what they should do next, some of them having only seen life at boarding school and were probably used to having exact instructions for everything. What they were missing is that the fact that there were no instructions was exactly the point. Clearly the test was to see what we would do in the circumstances.

I was in a militant mood so decided to

write an essay about how flawed the o 'level system was and how crap it would be that for the rest of my life I would be judged on how good my memory was on one single day.

For lunch we were shown in to the The Park canteen and told to select whatever we wanted. The next hour lunching with the geeks was probably the most painful 60 minutes of my life and nearly put me off proceeding with the interview, in case this was the life I was signing up to. I think if leaving had been an option I may well have taken it - as it happens there was nowhere to go and we were there until the end of the day. The geeks started talking to each other about the previous test and one even admitted leaving a blank piece of paper, another said he was annoyed because he didn't have enough paper to do his hobby, ham radio, full justice. I wanted to puke in my lunch.

The interview was a real experience. I walked into a room with a panel of four guys sat at a long table. They were all in their fifties or sixties and the guy on the end was puffing away at a pipe. They took it in turns to ask standard interview questions and then moved on to my personal life asking what I did in my spare time. The one with the pipe who hadn't said anything until now and looked as though he might fall asleep any minute then asked me what paper I read and who my favourite columnist was.

The truth was I didn't read any particular paper and had no idea what the name of any columnists were. I was just thinking how I might blag this when I remembered and realised now what the friendly guy who picked me up from the gatehouse was trying to help me with. I repeated what he said verbatim;

'I try and read The Times and my favourite columnist is the Foreign Affairs correspondent Richard Jenkins.'

'Excellent choice' quaffed Mr pipe smoker and wrote something down. I owed that guy a beer whoever he was.

'Thank you, you may leave now, if you would just wait outside you will be escorted to the mini bus shortly.'

I got up to leave when one of the others said

'One last question. Are you gay?'

I didn't know what to say and must have looked stunned before responding with;

'No of course not' I realised if one of them was gay I had just offended him.

'Then why do you wear an ear ring?'

I didn't really know how to answer that. The old buffoons clearly regarded men with earrings as an expression of gayness even though most people I knew had one. But then I don't suppose any of them had ever stepped foot in The Foresters Public House.

I was going to say something sarcastic but one of the others interjected.

'Leave him alone you old fool. The young chaps wear them these days.'

'Really? - Looks like a gay to me.'

Within minutes I was on the minibus home reflecting on the most bizarre day of my life so far.

One of the things that needed to take place in parallel with the interview process was something called positive vetting. At 17 I hadn't had much of a life to investigate yet but nevertheless I had to offer a teacher and a personal friend that I had known for a minimum of five years for the government to interview.

My head of form at Newland was happy to act as a reference and I gave my old mate Roger as a personal reference. It nearly ended right there.

Rog worked as a fishmongers assistant in Tottenham, North London. He told me that one Saturday afternoon he was out back filleting some Herring when Len, who's shop it was, called him out front.

'Kop a load of that!' Normally that phrase was reserved for a good looking bird in the queue (they had long queues on a Saturday) but today it was a bloke in a black suit with a briefcase and wearing of all things a bowler hat. As the guy got closer they were speculating as to what fish he was going to order when instead he asked;

'May I speak to Roger please?'

'Sure mate. ROG' Len shouted.

Roger appeared wearing his white fishmonger apron covered in fish blood wondering what he'd done. He knew the bloke wasn't a copper, and he looked like a taxman but Rog didn't earn enough to pay tax.

'Can I help you mate?'

'Yes, I'd like to discuss a friend of yours' to which he named me.

'Sure, but I don't have an office'

'Back there will do'

Astonishingly the guy sat down at the back of the fishmongers, and cool as a cucumber with no regard to the blood and stink surrounding him, proceeded to ask a series of questions. He started with the mundane such as how long have you known each other, what have you done together socially etc and the went in for the kill.

'Has he ever displayed any homosexual tendencies?'

Never missing an opportunity for a laugh Rog replied;

'Well there was the one time...'

'Let me stop you there. Everything you say will be a matter of record. If you are about to say that he has at some point expressed homosexual tendencies then it will be recorded as such and may affect his application.'

'Whoa mate just having a laugh'

'May I ask that you take this seriously and respond with either Yes or No.'

'Ok mate – No then,'

'Thank you.'

The man left. Rog was left wondering what had just happened and whether or not he'd just killed my application.

QUEEN AND COUNTRY

TWO

The Park 1982 - 1984 TRAINING

Survivor were at No 1 in the charts with 'Eye of the Tiger', Blade Runner was released in the cinema and British Forces had been successful in retaking the Falklands.

Somehow I had made it through the interview process and was one of eight trainees selected for the Training School. The two year training scheme was intense. It was mostly academic with some practical along the way and a series of exams at the end of the first year. The second year was spent going round the various OSD sections gaining experience in their specialties. The risks were fairly high because if you failed at any point you were out. No ifs or buts, just out. The problem with that was we were being taught about equipment and procedures that didn't exist in the real world and therefore if you didn't make it you would be two years older with nothing to show for it. Your mates would either be finishing A levels ready for University or two years into some form of apprenticeship.

Failure simply wasn't an option to consider.

We were told in no uncertain terms that we had to stay out of any kind of trouble and have squeaky clean personal lives during training or we were instantly out. There was no HR bullshit here, trainees did not have any employment rights. Despite having some dubious drinking buddies and the attendance at more than one footie match which had ended in near riot, I managed to stay out of any significant trouble - other than one regrettable incident. Blokes being blokes, we had various silly competitions, one of which was to see who could get through security at the main gate with the most ridiculous item. All staff were issued with blue photo passes which had to be shown whenever entering the site and whenever challenged but we suspected some of the older security guards didn't take much notice if they knew us or the car we were in. S, one of the more geeky trainees was winning the competition after getting in by flashing a Barclays Bank card.

I wasn't going to be beaten and after a traditional Friday lunchtime session at a local pub I took inspiration from the beermat my pint was on. I folded it and tore off strips until it was roughly the same size as my pass, it wasn't exactly the same blue but I thought it close enough. I was in the back of H's car along with S and as we slowed down at the main gate, H held up his pass, S held up his Barclaycard and I held up the beermat. The security guard waved us through and as we pulled into the Training School car park I smugly informed H and S that I was now leading the competition.

That afternoon I was summoned to the Head of Training School's office.

'Sit down Maedan.' I sat.

'Show me your pass.' I showed him my pass.

'All seems to be in order.' He smiled.

'So perhaps you can explain why you thought it was funny to show an unidentified item when entering this lunchtime.'

I thought about denying it but I could easily have been caught on camera so decided to just take what was coming. I said nothing.

'Do I need to remind you that we take security very seriously here and entering a high security government establishment without appropriate identification is serious offence.' Now he wasn't smiling.

'Strictly speaking I did have appropriate identification, I just didn't ..'

'I'd stop speaking now Maedan if I were

you. Go back to your training session and understand that this is now on your record. Any repeat shenanigans will result in instant dismissal.'

I joined the others in the classroom gutted not because I was in a bit of trouble but because due to the fact I was caught my attempt didn't count in the competition. What really pissed me off though was that they hadn't even noticed S's Barclaycard.

I passed the first year exams and somewhat relieved was looking forward to the section rotation. There were now seven trainees left as one guy failed his exams and we had learnt by then that The Park was pretty much divided into two departments, OSD and COD.

For me there was no question, Operational Security Department was without doubt the one to be in. It was OSD who did all the foreign travel and worked in Embassies around the world. It was also the OSD guys who got the three year postings overseas. If there was any fun, glamour, money and excitement it was OSD. COD or Communications Operations Division even sounded boring. Those guys were based in workshops at The Park doing the same stuff day after day. I always thought if you didn't want to travel then why not just go and get a real job rather than waste away in COD.

Of course as keen 17 year olds all the trainees wanted OSD but knew that previous trainees had always been split between the two departments upon graduation. The trick was to do well in your training time in the OSD sections and if possible get one to formally ask for you on completion of your training.

The only trouble was, the others all knew that too.

My year experiencing the various sections was relatively uneventful, we all knew we were there to learn and impress at the same time. OSD was everything. To me it was like two worlds, the cool guys of OSD leading exciting lifestyles and living a little on the edge and the more academic COD geek fest that did important work albeit from nine to five in the same department for thirty years.

One thing I realised fairly quickly was that most of the OSD guys were not that bothered about academic ability, they were looking for someone they wouldn't mind being stuck in an Eastern Bloc crap hole for two months with. I did my best to keep out of trouble, produce good work (in the OSD sections) and most importantly fit in with the banter. My love of real ale and football was probably the only edge I had over the geeks I was competing with for those OSD assignments. I also played a bit of a game myself by only producing my best work in OSD and deliberately acting disinterested in COD sections.

As it was an almost exclusively male environment, and many years before political correctness was even an expression, the banter could be harsh and having an earring was both a blessing and a burden. To some of the older guys I must have been gay and therefore not someone to be overseas with and to the younger guys there was a hint of rebel that they liked. Either way I was not going to be forgotten in a hurry.

The day we were graduating and getting our deployment letters was one of the most nervous I can remember. The other trainees, bar one notable exception, were all more academic than me and for some time I had resigned myself to a life in COD or even trying to find something in the real world. We were all sat together when we opened our letters.

When I saw the three magic letters OSD it was as much as I could do to stop myself from jumping around. I'm not sure who was the most surprised, me or the other trainees.

FINN MAEDAN

QUEEN AND COUNTRY

THREE

WARSAW JANUARY 1985
TRADE CRAFT

Dead or Alive were at No 1 with 'You Spin me Round', Back to the Future had just been released at the cinema and Clive Sinclair launched the C5 onto the streets of London.

I had just turned 20 and about to join my first permanent OSD section. It was 1985 and exciting times for the department as Cold War activity was at its height. The Russians had recently shot down a Korean Airline flight 007 from New York, claiming it had violated Soviet restricted airspace. 269 passengers and crew were killed including a member of US congress.

The Russians claimed it was on a spy mission and its mission was to deliberately provoke their defense systems. The US claimed the plane had made a genuine mistake by flying off course, either way the incident had raised tensions to an extremely high level. As a consequence our job had never been more important and never more in the spotlight.

I was getting to know the blokes in my team and slowly getting experience on the systems and equipment that my section used. I was also starting to work out how things worked politically, who the people to know were and who to avoid. I had also learnt the structure of the Department what the various sections were and the way most peoples' careers panned out. It seemed the way forward was to do short trips for a few years, keep your nose clean and then you would be offered a three year tour stationed in an Embassy overseas.

My particular section was run by D, a Senior Officer who had been in the job for around twenty years and had done two full tours overseas.

D was one of the good guys, he tried hard to be fair about the distribution of work and was always checking in on new recruits to see how they were getting on. He was usually found sat behind his desk until precisely 12.30 when he would go over to the on-site pub the Plug & Socket (no I'm not kidding) for his lunchtime pie and whisky.

It was almost a ritual that whenever he left for the Plug, the guys would pile into his office to check what was affectionately known as 'the Leader Board'. This was a magnetic white board that had all our names down the left hand side in blue and the months of the year across the top in red. The various planned trips, which were mostly installations of some sort, were simply place names stuck in the middle cross referencing a name against a date.

The Leader Board got its name from the guys who were convinced that the best jobs went to D's golfing buddies. For a number of reasons the board was often subject to change which is why it got so much attention whenever he left his office.

To this day I'm sure D moved things around for fun knowing we all rushed in there at lunchtimes.

One afternoon R from the CCTV section called into our workshop and asked me if my passport was valid and whether I fancied a trip abroad. It took less than a millisecond for me to respond in the positive – I was going on my first short trip.

He said that he needed to get special clearance because I was only 20 and he needed me to join him on an emergency job in Poland where there was a minimum age of 21 for OSD operatives. He said he didn't think it would be a problem because he knew the right people to get the clearance sorted. As I got to know R over the coming months, it became obvious he certainly did.

A few days later clearance came through, as did an emergency visa and the flights were booked for the following week. I was going to be the youngest person ever sent on a short mission to a communist country and I couldn't wait.

I was picked up early next Monday in a Park standard issue blue car, R already reading a paper on the back seat. We were on our way to Heathrow.

'Got your passport, toothbrush etc?' asked R.

'Sure have but I'll pick some toothpaste up at the airport.' R just laughed.

'You won't be seeing much of the airport.'

I had no idea what he was on about until about an hour or so later when we pulled up at a service entrance to Heathrow. The Park driver had a chat with the airport perimeter security guard and R showed him our passports. The guard gave the driver some directions, waved us through and I realised we were driving along the service road just in front of the actual aircraft.

Five minutes later, I found it hard to take in we were pulling up underneath the actual BA flight that was taking us to Warsaw. R got out and opened the boot of the car to retrieve a couple of suitcase sized diplomatic bags. Diplomatic bags were effectively hessian sacks with 'H.B.M. Diplomatic Service' written across them in large navy blue letters. They were gathered at the top and tightly tied with a string and lead seal. The international diplomatic code meant that dip bags must always be given free passage and could not be opened, manipulated or even x-rayed. The Park rules were that if you were escorting them, they were never to leave your sight.

R explained that standard procedure when carrying bags on aircraft was that we would watch them into the aircraft's hold and then board the plane ourselves while the Park driver stayed to keep an eye on the then closed hold until the plane took off. I could see other passengers looking at us wondering what the hell was going on as we were the last to board with the two front seats reserved for us. I don't mind admitting it made me feel quite important.

The flight was uneventful and on arrival at Warsaw International Airport, the stewardesses arranged for us to be the first off. We walked down the stairs to the tarmac where an Embassy vehicle was waiting, the driver already supervising the unloading of the hold. Minutes later we were through Pilot customs and on our way to the Embassy. No wait, no fuss. I was starting to like this diplomatic travel lark.

We dumped the equipment off at the Embassy and proceeded to check in at the Forum Hotel who were expecting us. R suggested to meet in the hotel bar in an hour. I walked into the bar and spotted R already sat at a table with two beers. He said I would be learning a few ground rules that evening and we would start with a meal in the hotel restaurant followed by a walk to grab a beer somewhere. It all sounded good to me.

Keen to experience the local food I ordered a cold beetroot soup followed by Wild Boar and dumplings. Over dinner R asked me what I had noticed about the hotel bar earlier. My vacant look clearly gave him the impression I didn't know what he meant so he tried to help.

'Did you not notice the number of stunning women that were in there?'

'Sure, I suppose so?'

'Well didn't you think that odd? Was it anything like your normal drinking hole?'

'I thought back to The Foresters in Stony – he had a good point.

He smiled. 'They are nearly all prostitutes and the ones that aren't work for the Polish Secret Service. Believe me if they talk to you they only want your money or your information. Either way don't go anywhere near them as many a career has been blighted in that very bar.'

He leaned forward and started to whisper. 'The other thing to know is that all of the rooms are bugged and some are even fitted with cameras. We don't know which rooms have the cameras so the best thing to do is always assume it's your room and act accordingly.'

It was all sounding very James Bond like at this point which to a 20 year old was music to my ears.

After we'd finished eating and were ready to go for a beer R said to watch closely as I was about to get lesson 1. Discretely holding out three folded twenty dollar US bills, he asked the waiter for the check and whether he could pay in US dollars. The waiter looked around sheepishly before nodding and taking the money. Five minutes later he came back with an oversized receipt on his tray that was resting on top of two piles of Polish Zlotys, the local currency. R took the wedges of local cash and in a move Paul Daniels would have been proud of discreetly placed them in his jacket pocket.

'See what happened there?'

'I'm guessing you changed your dollars into Zlotys'

'Wrong. That would be illegal. I asked if I could pay in dollars and because I didn't have the right money he chose to give me my change in Zlotys. At no point did I ask to change my money. Which by the way is at a rate 5 times better than the official government rate.'

Clever old bastard knew all the tricks.

We went for a walk through the narrow

cobbled streets of Warsaw's Old Town and found a small bar where we stopped for a couple of beers. We hadn't been there long when R suggested moving on to another bar round the corner which he had been to on previous trips.

Arriving at the next bar, R ordered a couple of beers and chose a table for us to sit at.

He leaned forward and asked; 'Without making it obvious, do you notice anything odd?'

I waited a couple of minutes and pretended to look at a sign above the bar while quickly scanning the room.

'Not really no.'

'The guy drinking a beer at the end of the bar in a light coat was at the last bar we were in.'

R had deliberately sat opposite a mirror that allowed him to take the room in without any tell-tale neck movements.

'I suspect he is assigned to be our company for the evening. Drink up and we'll find out.'

We left the bar and walked back towards the hotel. We were about two streets away from the hotel when R chirped up with;

'One for the road?' Before I could even reply he had one foot inside a little pub-like bar he'd spotted.

R ordered three beers.

'Three?

'Wait a while. You'll see.'

Around thirty minutes later R said;

'See why I got three now?

I had a look around and gave him a puzzled look.

'Jesus I need to work on you' He got up and took the drink to a man wearing a dark coat and hat at the bar. The man didn't look too pleased and got up and left. As he walked passed me on his way out I noticed it was the same guy as earlier although he'd changed his coat and now had a hat.

'Seems he wasn't in the mood for a drink tonight' smiled R.

More like he was gutted that he'd been spotted. There was no fooling an old fox like R.

R then briefed me on a few other operational principles. He explained that we didn't really communicate with those at home when we were in an Eastern Bloc country. We were allowed to send a postcard but it could not be posted locally and would instead be sent in the diplomatic mail to London where it would be transferred to the Royal Mail. The postcard could display the city we were in but the text would be read in London and the postcard destroyed if it gave away any details as to the work we were doing or the team we were with.

Sending postcards this way made a nice souvenir for your parents but it was effectively useless as often you would get home before the postcard. It was, in extreme situations, possible to send information by encrypted telegram (the way Embassies communicated in the days before the internet) but only for very serious matters. As an 'essential weekly test' of the system, all Embassies received the football results by secure telegram from The Park on a Saturday evening.

R also warned me that as a new boy I might be subject to the local secret service mind games when I go back to my room. Typical scenarios were to have a poo waiting in the loo or a burning cigarette in an ashtray. Sometimes if married, a new favourite was to lay the wife's underwear out on the bed. It was well-known that they wanted to show you that they could come and go as they pleased to unsettle you, but because we were trained to deal with these things and therefore ignore them, in recent times attention had been switched to wives. They knew that if they could cause disruption and grief at home you would be less effective in the workplace.

I went back to my room but there was nothing untoward. I was secretly hoping to find something just so that I could talk about it the next day but as hard as I searched I couldn't find a thing.

Perhaps they thought they didn't need to do

anything to make me any less effective at work.

QUEEN AND COUNTRY

FOUR

LISBON FEBRUARY 1985
THE RESTAURANT

Elaine Page was at No 1 with 'I know him so well', The Goonies was released at the cinema and Miners called off their year long strike.

The Portuguese love the English. Well that's what I was told by the guys working in the Lisbon Embassy. Apparently they call us 'the oldest ally' which is a reference to some fight against the French in Napoleonic times. Seemed to me as though a lot of water had gone under the bridge since then but if they wanted to love us that was fine with me.

There were three of us out in Lisbon and it's probably the hardest I've ever had to work. K needed to get back for a wedding or something and therefore wanted to squeeze a six week job into three. His plan was to take advantage of the long lunch times when the Embassy was deserted so that we could do our disruptive work and then again when people left in the evening. We literally had a 30 minute break from around 8am to 9pm every day.

Not so as to break with the OSD work hard play harder ethos, after packing up we would go back to the room for a quick shower and then hit the bars.

One evening J, the Embassy Registrar invited us to join her and some of the others for a meal out. It was always smart to stay on the good side of Registry staff so K reluctantly agreed to pack up early and join them.

We met at a typical local 'hole in the wall'. A Portuguese restaurant that had virtually no signage but was well known to locals and was literally an old wooden door in a stone mediaeval building that once you stepped inside was a bit of a Tardis.

The owner was clearly expecting us and beckoned that we sit at a table for 12 he had already prepared.

The owner said something to the group in Portuguese and to all of our surprise J, the Registrar, replied also in fluent Portuguese. We sat down and ordered a round of cocktails while K perused the wine menu. Predictably he threw out his 'when in Rome' line and ordered four bottles of Portuguese wine.

The waitress returned with the four bottles, opened one for us and let K taste it before opening the other three bottles. She placed the bill on a metal spike in the middle of the table.

Another four bottles later the owner, a small, fat, red faced man probably in his fifties came over to the table, said something in Portuguese and then pointed to a small bar complete with optics, at the back of the restaurant. We were all looking to see what he was pointing at when he lifted the previous bills off the spike and started rolling them into a ball. He then proceeded to eat them.

When he had swallowed the lot he said something again in Portuguese and walked off. Dismayed, we all looked at each other and then to J for an explanation.

J explained that he had said that all drinks were on him and from now on we would be served from his personal bar reserved for friends and family.

A few people cheered but I was a little bothered by the situation. I pointed out to J that now the owner had eaten the bill he could charge us anything he wanted and we wouldn't know what we'd had. She didn't seem concerned.

As the evening went on we all ordered food from the menu and many more bottles of wine came to the table. I made a point of watching where the waitress was getting drinks from and she had indeed been getting them from the owners 'personal' bar. By the end of the evening we'd polished off a three course meal each, countless bottles of wine, numerous cocktails and a few short drinks. I told J we should start to gather some money because anything could happen when it came to the bill. She said I was worrying needlessly but agreed and I guessed at around £30 per head which would have been about right. Everyone coughed up the cash and I had the kitty waiting for the eventual bill.

An hour later, full to bursting and tipsy to say the least, we were contemplating calling it a night when the owner came over brandishing a couple of bottles.

A couple of people had stood up to leave and he motioned them to sit back down as he repeated his party trick of waving the overall bill at us before shoving it into his mouth and eating it. Here we go I thought.

He turned to J and gabbled away dramatically in Portuguese with lots of hand movements. As he was speaking two of his staff came over and put a port glass in front of each one of us. He then walked round the table filling each glass continuing his speech which by now was even more dramatic. When he had finished his circle of the table, he poured himself a glass, held it up and finished his speech with a loud 'Salute!'

He walked off leaving a bottle and a half of

vintage port on the table.

Everyone was keen to know what on earth had just happened and there was an anticipating quiet while J prepared to recount what he had said. She told his story.

'His name is Marco. As a young man he was always running out of breath and struggled with even light work. This disappointed his father who thought he was lazy and would ruin the family restaurant which he would be inheriting one day. To compound things he started to put on weight and his father introduced him to others as the family pig. Five years ago his father passed away leaving him the restaurant but very soon afterwards he collapsed and was rushed to hospital. The Lisbon General Hospital diagnosed him as having a rare heart defect but were unable to operate on him. A British surgeon heard about the anomaly and because he was fascinated in the case offered to fly in and operate at no cost. He designed a way to fix Marco's heart and explained the risks of operating using a procedure that had not been attempted before.

The operation was a complete success and now Marco is happy, healthy and runs a thriving restaurant. He will forever be in the debt of England and her Queen and is very proud to have representatives of the British Embassy in his restaurant who will never pay for their food or wine.'

It was a great story and there was the odd teary eye as I handed back everyone's £30.

Me and K raised a glass to the anonymous surgeon and felt no guilt as we finished off the vintage Port.

FIVE

The Park MARCH 1985
MILLWALL

Dead or Alive were at No 1 with 'You Spin me Round', Back to the Future had just been released at the cinema and Gorbachev became the Soviet Leader.

I'm quite a private person really. I'm not sure exactly why that is but I suspect being brought up with 5 sisters and then a job which at the time was not allowed to be talked about has something to do with it. Add to that constantly travelling and never being able to commit to time with friends or even playing for a football team and it could be quite a lonely existence at times. It's probably also why I can count my true friends on one hand, mainly because they would have to put up with me not contacting them, not showing up for important occasions etc (I'm still rubbish at contacting people).

In March 1985 one of my oldest friends R, asked me to go to a football match with him. He was a lifelong Millwall fan and they had been drawn in the FA Cup at Luton, a relatively easy ground to get to from Milton Keynes. I wasn't a fan of either club and although I knew getting into trouble could be the end of my short-lived OSD career, Luton was a family club not known for its fans and there wasn't any trouble expected.

When we got to Luton's ground it was chaos outside as many more Millwall fans had turned up than the police expected. As a consequence only a small section of the ground had been made available with three turnstiles and police on horses attempting to hold the queues of fans back. Although Luton were asked by Millwall to make the Wednesday night match all-ticket, the warning wasn't heeded and it turned out that a disproportionately large away following, twice the size of Millwall's average home gate, arrived on the day of the game.

By 5.00 pm pubs and newsagents around the town were having windows smashed as the police struggled to cope. The Kenilworth Stand, at that time still a vast terrace, was reserved for the away supporters that night but it was full by 7pm – 45 minutes before kick-off. To make it worse the turnstiles had been broken down. Ten minutes later, the police were helpless as hundreds of the visitors scaled the fences in front of the stand to escape the crush and started to mass menacingly along the side of the pitch.

The inevitable became a reality and some fans rushed down the pitch towards Luton's supporters in the packed Oak Road End. A hail of bottles, cans, nails and coins saw the home supporters fleeing up the terraces, but their numbers, still growing as fans entered the stand, meant that there was nowhere to go.

The trouble then spread to the Bobbers Stand, where seats were ripped out and used as weapons. A message appeared on the stadium's electronic scoreboard, stating that the match would not start until Millwall fans returned to their allocated area, but this was ignored. It was only when George Graham appeared on the side line that the spectators finally returned to the Kenilworth Stand.

As the game entered its final stages, with Millwall now losing the rumour was going round that the pitch may be invaded once more in order to have the match abandoned and therefore prevent a defeat. Fans attempted to disrupt the match, but extra police managed to keep control.

Following the final whistle, and a 1–0 victory for Luton, the Millwall fans invaded the pitch. The seats ripped from the stand were hurled onto the pitch towards the police, who started to fall back, before regrouping and charging in waves, batons drawn.

Me and R had been forced by the rush of the crowd onto the pitch although R wasn't complaining.

As we were running across the pitch an orange plastic seat came flying through the air and hit me on the head. The blow was enough to briefly knock me out, maybe for a minute or two, and when I came round R was dragging me by one arm towards the advertising hoards at the side of the pitch. The police had regrouped again and were now baton charging the Millwall fans who were retreating into the terrace.

The police stopped on the pitch at the bottom of the terrace. We were standing on the terrace looking down at the police and just as I was thinking it was probably over, the guy to my left picked up a broken seat and launched it at the nearest copper. Unfortunately for me, he was standing too close to me to get the angle he wanted and it scraped me across the face as he threw it.

I now had a scratch right the way down my left cheek and blood dripping down from the cut on my head I received earlier. The police made a final baton charge up the terrace forcing the remaining fans towards an exit.

Around 10 minutes later having walked down a Luton street with battered cars and houses with smashed windows, we jumped on a bus heading back to Milton Keynes. There were a group of Millwall fans at the back of the bus who saw the state of me and started clapping as if I was some kind of war veteran. Not for the first time that evening, R was just laughing.

The next day I was worried about work finding out where I'd been the previous night. I walked in to the workshop and after fielding a few questions about the scratch by saying it was my mum's cat, I thought it had gone pretty well until D called me in to his office.

He had the Daily Express in front of him and turned it over. There was a huge picture of fans running across the pitch on the back page. He looked at me and said;

'It's a good job you weren't involved in that. Could have been very difficult for you.'

'Now go back to the workshop and tell M I want to see him.' As I was leaving he said;

'Oh and tell your mum to get her cat's nails clipped.' He wasn't smiling.

QUEEN AND COUNTRY

SIX

KHARTOUM OCTOBER 1985
TWENTY ONE

Jennifer Rush was at No 1 with 'The Power of Love', The Breakfast Club was the big movie release and a policeman was killed horrifically in the Tottenham Riots.

The previous day had been seen the incident with D trying to run the check point on the way to the airport (see prologue). So far it seemed as though word hadn't got back to anyone about D's exploits. With that hanging over us and no end in sight to the coup, things were a bit subdued to say the least. We had finished the job we came out to do and just wanted to go home.

D had somehow explained the state of the bullet riddled Embassy Cortina and no doubt left out the bits where he drunkenly ran the check point. The MI6 guy had retreated into his secure area probably traumatised for life and certainly not to be seen by us again. It was two days until my 21st birthday and although that isn't a big a deal as it used to be in my parents day, it's still a fairly big occasion and I had all sorts of plans to go out with the lads back home and get smashed. I was now starting to think I was going to be stuck here in Khartoum with nothing to do and because Sudan was a dry country, nowhere to go other than the Embassy bar.

We were staying in the Khartoum Hilton which was nice enough. It was clean, had air conditioning and a bizarre buffet every night that was exactly the same food but somehow dressed differently to be Indian night, Chinese night or Tex-Mex night.

It also had an underground bowling alley which was totally unexpected in the middle of Sudan and you knew when the BA crew were staying over because the bowling alley would be packed full of Sudanese standing around watching the stewardesses tottering around trying to bowl.

I was watching the TV in the room when CNN announced that the military coup in Sudan was now over, the army had seized power and that international flights would be running shortly. It looked like I might get to leave after all, albeit on my actual birthday. The next day we headed straight to the airport hoping they would honor our existing tickets.

I remember boarding the BA flight, taking my economy seat and thinking I was lucky a) because I was leaving b) because the tiny overhead screen was only about four seats away from me and c) D was sat a few rows behind where I didn't have to speak to him.

About an hour into the flight, I had settled in and enjoying a beer when a stewardess tapped me on the shoulder told me the captain wanted a word. I recognized her as one of the bowling attractions. I didn't know what was going on but that isn't something you can turn down really. She showed me to a seat in First Class and said;

'Happy Birthday Sir, compliments of BA.'

She returned with the Captain and two glasses of champagne and sat next to me. The Captain went on to explain that the Embassy had called to tell them that due to the trouble in Khartoum I'd been delayed leaving and would now be spending my 21st on their flight. As that was a pretty rare way to spend your 21st, BA had decided to upgrade me. Better still because a number of the flight crew had also been stuck in Khartoum the Captain had given them permission to have a glass of champagne with me every time we crossed a time zone where I would be 21 again.

Sadly there were only another two time zones.

QUEEN AND COUNTRY

SEVEN

WARSAW APRIL 1986
CHERNOBYL

George Michael was at No 1 with 'A Different Corner', Aliens was the smash hit at the cinema and a bomb had blown a hole in the side of a TWA aircraft over Greece.

A year on from my first ever overseas job I was returning to Warsaw. Now 21, I didn't need special permission and was on a three man team tasked with fitting a state of the art CCTV system that had built in motion detection zones on certain cameras.

The Embassy then was an old palace with huge stately rooms and passages behind fireplaces. It had a large open courtyard, a baroque facade and ornate balustrade surrounding the lower roof sections. One afternoon me and H were running cables along the roof to a camera that had been mounted on a chimney stack. It was fairly precarious as there was no way you were surviving a fall onto the courtyard so we had climber's harnesses on and were tied to the roof hatch. If we fell we would be dangling over the edge. Not great but not dead.

We spent the afternoon terminating the cables and testing the camera telemetry systems and then using walkie talkies adjusted them based on the view that the security guards had on their monitors.

At around 6 we called it a day and went straight into the Embassy bar for a well-earned beer. No cash was allowed to be taken and the payment system was tokens which you could purchase from the Embassy but we would usually just run up a tab and pay at the end of the job. That evening the bar was manned by J one of the Embassy Security guards who was ex Commando and for whatever reason took a shine to us never adding our beers to the tab.

Poland being under strict communist rule and with espionage attacks at their height, Embassy bars were regarded as 'safe' places to drink and relax so the western community, which out there was the US, Italy, the Aussies and of course us, had agreed to have 2 for 1 nights on different nights of the week so that each could visit the others. There were always a couple of Aussies in the Brit bar but that night there were also four off duty US marines.

I was standing at the bar listening to one of J's many Commando stories when a huge black marine tapped me on the shoulder.

'Where you from man?'

'London.' We were from Milton Keynes but there was never any point saying that to an American.

'London, Canada?'

I looked at him as if he was nuts.

'No – London, England.'

'You shitting me man?'

'No – I'm British'

'Thought you just said you were English' I looked at him puzzled. Was he taking the piss? J was pissing himself laughing.

'So – If you're British where did y'all learn to speak Canadian?' He was actually serious.

'Go sit down five you fuckwit' piped up J still laughing.

The marine simply said 'good evening gentlemen' and went back to his buddies.

'America's finest. Stupid fuckers aren't they? And that ones in charge!' said J washing a beer mug.

'Watch this. Oi Four' he shouted.

Two marines turned to acknowledge him.

'Yo, sup J-man'

'Sorry fellas, I meant three' the other Marine sat with them said;

'Can I help you sir'

'Was just wondering if you needed another round. It's yours next isn't it?' Knowing full well it wasn't.

'Hell no - five's up next.'

'Sure am' responded the big black marine.

'Ok boys - beers on the way' J started pouring.

'What's going on with the numbers?' I whispered to J.

'Believe it or not it's their life expectancy in minutes should the US Embassy be attacked. The ones with the lowest numbers are nearest the Embassy gates. The fuckwits are proud of it. Watch this.' J then rang a bell and shouted out the word 'numbers'.

The marines jumped to attention, rolled one sleeve up each to reveal a marine corps tattoo with their life expectancy number underneath and shouted 'ooh-rah' in unison.

J was laughing. 'That's just cost you a round son. It's tradition for a new face in the bar or 'on deck' as that lot call it.' Trying not to laugh at this demonstration of US military might, I was happy to get the round in.

'Good fucking grief' said H turning back to his pint.

A while later one of the Embassy staff came running into the bar saying we should check the news. There was a small black & white portable TV on the end of the bar tuned to a local Polish TV station. A few of us were watching a reporter talking with a picture behind of him of what looked like a power station but none of us knew what was being said.

J switched on a radio which was tuned to World Service for the football results but had now interrupted programs for a special news bulletin.

A nuclear reactor in Chernobyl Russia had exploded and there was a cloud of radioactive pollution making its way across Europe. We didn't really know what any of this meant but it was obviously serious and the Russians were not exactly forthcoming with information, in fact so far it was Swedish scientists who had detected the radiation and reported it to the press.

The Ambassador called Senior Staff to a briefing room in the Embassy, including my boss G.

Those at the meeting were told that staff should remain indoors for the time being until further information was available and should be advised to use only frozen or tinned foods. Countries on the high risk list included Poland.

The next day there was chaos. Hundreds of British citizens living in Poland had turned up at the Embassy looking for advice and wanting help to get a flight home. All flights were now booked solid for two weeks and there were rumors going round that aircraft may have to be grounded until more was known about the radioactive cloud.

The Embassy staff had been given their instructions to tell families to stay indoors and morale was starting to drop particularly amongst the female members of staff. As more information came through the various news channels, one thing was evident – the cloud had already passed over Poland and worse, we were working on the roof at the time.

The next day the Embassy agreed a deal with BA to get all wives and children flown back to the UK but asked the secretaries to volunteer to stay behind. Most did and a few left.

Whitehall decided to send a team of scientists out to take readings of any airborne radiation and to check local milk and vegetables. They turned up at the Embassy and started unpacking their equipment when the Head of Chancery, (second to the Ambassador) came up with the brainwave of getting them to use their Geiger counter to check all staff. I thought this was likely to be a no win situation and a potential PR disaster. If the readings were high were they going to tell people? And if the readings were normal would anyone believe them?

We volunteered to go first and were told the readings were higher than normal but not anything to panic about. I remember the most disconcerting thing being the ticking of the instrument they used to check us which went ballistic as it was being scanned over our bodies – according to them only a normal noise and what it was supposed to do. I suggested to my boss that this would freak the secretaries out and he quietly approached one of the scientists to ask if they would turn the audio off when scanning them. They refused.

No surprise to us that evening there was almost mutiny as the secretaries having been scanned and freaking out at the meaningless results all demanded to be sent home. In an effort to keep calm the Ambassador promised to contact BA and see what he could arrange. Morale was awful with female staff openly crying at their desks as more and more rumors were circulating including one about radiation levels damaging their ability to have children.

Myself and J decided we would do something to try and cheer people up. The Ambassador was away travelling to another part of Poland so we organised a sit down meal to be held in his residence that night for all remaining secretaries and anyone else who wanted to join us. Beans on toast exhausted my cooking potential but J was good and could knock a decent meal up with any old ingredients. We asked staff to donate whatever they didn't want from their freezers and there was enough to do a makeshift Spaghetti Carbonara with ham and mushrooms. J set about doing the cooking and

I had an idea to add a bit of fun to the occasion.

We got everyone settled around the table at around 7, filled up the wine glasses and went to the kitchen to get the trays laden with bowls of Carbonara. I had earlier retrieved from the on-site workshop, a couple of paper all in one jumpsuits (the sort forensics wear), arctic gloves and eye goggles. Me and J got changed into the gear, rang what must have been the Ambassador's meal bell and walked in serving the food looking like a couple of extras from a contamination film. Luckily the room erupted with laughter. One thing the Brits are good at is taking the piss out of themselves and situations they are in. The food was surprisingly good and the wine and champagne was in abundance, so for that night at least people could forget what was going on around them.

The following morning the Ambassador asked to see the three of us. He said he had heard about the antics of the previous evening, including a rumored competition to see who could hit his paintings with a champagne cork (which was true, it was 10 points for every grand master you could hit) but that aside he was very grateful for our attempts to keep morale up. Some weeks later I found out that he even went to the lengths of writing to The Park to praise our actions, which was probably the only time something good ended up on my record.

A week later things had calmed down and the press were starting to report facts rather than rumor. We had finished the job we came out to do and made arrangements to return to the UK. We were carrying a few dip bags so arranged with The Park to have a minibus waiting on the tarmac. When we landed we followed standard protocol, were the first to depart the plane and went underneath to meet the driver. I noticed that as well as a minibus there was also one of the The Park Vauxhall Cavaliers.

'What's the car for' enquired J.

'You lot – didn't anyone tell you?' replied the driver.

'Tell us what?'

'You three are being taken straight to Kings Cross Hospital for tests'

'Brilliant – so good of those tossers to let us know'

'Oh and take your suitcases – they want your clothes too.'

We were then taken straight to Kings Cross Hospital where we were met by some form of consultant. Two big guys in civilian clothes took our suitcases and we were all taken down to the basement. The basement was clearly the last place for any decorating budget and looked as though it was a left over from Victorian times with tiled walls and peeling paint on the ceilings. We were shown into a small room and asked firstly to identify all clothes we had worn outside when working on the Embassy roof. The two burly guys bagged the clothes up and left. We were then asked to strip to our underwear for a few tests. One by one we went into another small room that had a large glass viewing window.

Tellingly the consultant stayed outside, shut the door and shouted instructions through the window. I had to stand on a cross made with masking tape on the floor while he remotely controlled what looked like a moving hat stand with a large metal cylinder bolted to it. It looked like a lab experiment more than a professional piece of medical equipment but he was able to manipulate it so that it came up to me and then raised the cylinder to key points on my body. The contraption took readings at my thigh, underarm and neck before he shouted through that I was done and could get dressed again. After we'd all been done we were told to wait until cleared to leave. About an hour later we were told we could go.

The next day at work we were recounting the story to our co-workers when D called us into his office. J was quite angry at the lack of information and he wanted to know the results of the tests and what was happening to our clothes. D said that our clothes had been taken to Aldermaston Army base for testing and would not be returned but we could apply for compensation. As to the tests, he had no information but would do what he could to find out.

All three of us put compensation claims in and in true government style the response came back that we needed receipts and the clothes value would be depreciated based on how old they were.

It was a joke really because no one keeps receipts for clothes and by the time they worked out how a pair of jeans devalues in three years we were offered a pittance. I was just gutted that my favourite 'Joe Cool' Snoopy t-shirt would never be seen again.

A year later we received a letter each telling us the results of the tests they did. Apparently there were 'interesting' (not a technical or medical term I have ever heard before) levels of radiation including a presence of isotopes including Cesium 55 which they hadn't expected and has a half-life of 30 years.

To this day I have no idea whether the results were good, bad or indifferent but I have fathered three children and none have webbed feet.

QUEEN AND COUNTRY

EIGHT

TEL AVIV JUNE 1986
WHITE POWDER

Dr & The Medics were at No 1 with 'Apirit in the Sky', Ferris Bueller's Day Off was the must see at the cinema and Richard Branson set a new trans-atlantic record in his powerboat Atlantic Challenger.

I was really looking forward to visiting Israel as I'd heard it was a fascinating place to visit with a unique mix of cultures and people that lived on the edge of their seats knowing that the next skirmish with a neighbor was just around the corner. It is perhaps their history of persecution and conflict that make the Israelis the people they are with an unfaltering deep pride for their country and a sense of living life to the full while you can.

The team for this visit was myself, P and J

with me being the most junior in both grade and age. We had been briefed before leaving that this might be an interesting one as relations with Syria were tense and Mossad (the Israeli Secret Service) were suspicious of the UK's stance. There had been reports of heightened activity in terms of the Embassy's intruder systems going off at night for no apparent reason, as well as strangers approaching Embassy personnel in bars making friendly but suspicious conversation – both classic Mossad practices.

On arrival we were introduced to the various Embassy staff who had, as was standard procedure, all been briefed of our arrival. An Embassy can have representatives from all sorts of government departments and most had MI6 operatives, Tel Aviv was no exception. The FCO rule was that no one should ever point out or refer to the MI6 staff on post. Words like 'spooks' were banned but they knew that on some occasions the subject had to come up and therefore the acceptable term to be used in conversation was 'friends'. We were not usually briefed as to who the 'friends' on site were until we got there and only then we would only be made aware on a 'need to know' basis as it was essential that in the vast majority of cases their true role was kept secret even from other Embassy staff. On the odd occasion, the MI6 operative was disclosed to the host country Secret Service, usually because they were working together on sensitive matters and it saved playing silly hunt the spook games.

The MI6 Head of Station was one of those disclosed roles and this guy T was a real character. He was larger than life in many ways, had a shock of white Einstein like hair and the last thing you would imagine him as walking down the street was a senior MI6 agent.

One morning T stopped me and P in passing in the Embassy corridor and asked us to join him in the Safe Room. The Safe Room was an enclosure in the core of the Embassy that was totally cut off electronically and acoustically from the outside world. It was the one place that you were assured of having a secure conversation or that was the theory anyway. T shut the heavy door behind us and we sat down at the meeting table. He explained a little bit about the current political situation and said that although he had a great relationship with Mossad they didn't believe he was disclosing everything regarding the UK's position on recent political events and that they would be ramping up direct espionage attacks on the Embassy.

He went on to say he was convinced they had been in his office on numerous occasions.

That revelation shocked us because you typically only heard that kind of thing in Eastern Europe and there was almost always some kind of evidence to give you reason to believe it. In this case there was no evidence and when you take into account the fact his office had no windows, was in a walled off area secured by a combination vault door, inside another Embassy area that secured by another huge metal vault door with a combination lock on not to mention an intruder detection system that had sensors in every corridor and on every door recording all activities, it all sounded a bit unrealistic. Nevertheless T was convinced.

Part of our job was to check over the Intruder Detection system, make sure it hadn't been tampered with and confirm that it was functioning correctly.

We would typically check for physical signs of access to the systems control unit and sensors, check all system logs for any suspicious activity at odd times and then run a full system test. We had to run the full system test at night so that it was only us around and we would exit all areas, alarm the system and then try and get back in undetected. If the system was setup properly every door we opened would trigger an activity in the log and every sensor in the corridor would catch us trying to sneak past. The only way we knew of to beat the system would be to nobble the sensors or nobble the log so that it didn't record any activities.

That evening we ran the full test. We

waited for all to leave, including T and his team and then set about locking and alarming from the inside out. We started with T's area and made sure all cabinets and safes were locked before leaving the area, locking the big vault door behind us and alarming the system. One of us would always double check the other had locked up properly.

We carried on doing this to the various areas, doors and corridors working our way out of the building until we left the final secure area door and set the system. We then proceeded to re-enter the building attempting to get past sensors by using potential blind spots. When we finished working our way back to the core we studied the event logs and as expected every door and every sensor had alarmed with a time stamp that exactly matched our route back in. The system was working perfectly.

That night after locking up again, confident that the Intruder Detection system was doing its job we went to a local bar for a few beers. The local beer was great and most of the bars were heaving, we couldn't believe how lively Tel Aviv was on a Wednesday night. With pumping music and young people having a great time, it could have been a bar in London until I saw something that was an instant reminder we were in a completely different culture.

Two young Israeli girls were standing at

the bar chatting to each other all glammed up in short skirts and high heels but with one thing that made them stand out immediately. They both had an Uzi sub machine gun over their shoulder.

To me it was a surreal sight almost like something out of a movie and J decided we had to go and talk to them and ask about the guns. It turned out they were off duty soldiers and one of the things they were encouraged to do was take their unloaded weapon everywhere they went. They went on to explain this was mainly for familiarity reasons as Israeli women soldiers had to 'get used to their Uzi as if it was a handbag' and also because they were on such heightened alert. They were effectively moments away from war with every nation that bordered them, and therefore wherever they are and whatever they were doing they could be called upon.

The theory was that because they had weapons with them they would just need to be supplied with ammunition which was strategically placed around the country. They also told us that it was every Israeli citizens duty to give a lift to a soldier requesting one meaning they had the ability to mobilise the entire country within minutes. I had a new found admiration for the Israeli army.

The next morning we got a call at the hotel to go in straight away because there had been an incident overnight. We rushed in and the

Head of Registry told us that T wanted to see us in his area as soon as possible. T was standing behind his desk pointing at a small mound of white powder on the carpet roughly in middle of his office floor.

'What do you make of that? Told you the fuckers were getting in.'

We were stunned. T assured us it was there when he walked in that morning. We knew we were the last to leave and I was 100% sure it wasn't there then as we would have noticed it. P went off to get the ID system logs and me and J tried to find an obvious source. It very much looked like the plaster powder you get from drilling residue which I had seen before but the only way that would be possible was if a hole had been drilled directly above it in the ceiling but that looked untouched.

For Mossad to have gotten in past the entire ID system, drill a hole in the ceiling plant a device of some sort and then hide any trace seemed totally implausible but it got there somehow so now we had a full investigation on our hands.

We only had limited equipment and T didn't want us to alert the UK until we had finished checking ourselves so we did what we could. We had a metal detector with us, normally used for finding wires in walls and we were able to check whether any listening devices were broadcasting. We put a radio on in the room tuned to Radio 4 and J fired up his kit. He went through the various frequency spectrums trying to detect a possible device broadcast. I went to the floor above to see if there was anything visible directly above the ceiling. A couple of hours later we sat down in the secure room with a coffee scratching our heads. The ID system logs showed us leaving following our testing the night before and T coming in the following morning. There was nothing in-between.

The metal detector found nothing and there was no evidence whatsoever of any drilling or tampering of any kind either in the ceiling above the dust pile or the floor the other side. J's report was no more useful, having scanned all frequency ranges there was no broadcast coming from T's office area. The entire thing was a complete mystery.

We decided that all we could do was take photographs and send them back to the UK with a sample of the powder which could be checked to see if it was the same composition as the ceiling plaster.

We went into T's area to take the various pictures of the scene only to find that the dust pile was gone.

P asked T's assistant what had happened and she had no idea. T had gone to an external meeting. We took pictures of the rest of the room in any case and the floor where the dust had been but that was now spotless as if the dust was never there.

Later when T returned to the office we caught up with him to ask what had happened to the dust pile.

'It was pissing me off so I binned it on my way out earlier.'

I couldn't believe what I was hearing. He had just scooped whatever it was up and shoved it in some public dustbin outside the Embassy. We could only fill in a SitRep (Situation Report) and send photos of a space on a carpet where something had once been which would make us look a bit silly.

That day left many questions unanswered for me. What was the dust? How did it get there? If the Israelis had been in and successfully concealed a device would they really forget to clean up? Was it just a message to say they can get in whenever they want to? And most puzzling of all, why did T get rid of the evidence? I will probably never know the answers.

QUEEN AND COUNTRY

NINE

TEL AVIV JUNE 1986
RECONNAISSANCE TRIP

With the 'dust' incident still bugging me it was a welcome respite when the Embassy's MOD representative asked me if I fancied a day out on the Jeep doing a reconnaissance trip to the Syrian border. J approved it saying they could do without me for the day so I set off with Captain S who was in his full army uniform. He told me that we were going on a routine reccy mission to the Syrian border which was two or three hours away depending on traffic and checkpoints. The Israelis allowed our military to travel freely as long as full documentation was carried and so all I needed was my diplomatic passport.

The Land Rover Jeep was probably the most uncomfortable vehicle I've ever been in for that length of time but the scenery on the road to Syria more than made up for it. We eventually reached a check point not too far from the border and pulled over as requested. The Israeli soldier asked for our papers and asked S what his business was. S told him we had to liaise with a Israeli Battalion that were in the area to attend a meeting, which of course was just bullshit. The soldier gave S a piece of paper and waved him through the checkpoint. S passed me the paper and asked me to take a look. It was a list of road names in blue followed by more road names in red. S explained that it was to tell him the approved routes we could travel freely in and those that he was not allowed to use.

'What colour is the 918 to Shamir?' asked S.

'Red'

'Thought it would be – oh well'

'Doesn't that mean we can't go that way?'

'Like fuck it does. It means we're not supposed to go that way which is an entirely different thing.' We headed down the 918.

He pulled over beside the road and stopped the Jeep. In the distance was a large hill with a white fenced off set of buildings on top surrounded by a couple of tall arial masts. S told me that it was an Israeli listening post that was in a highly restricted area which we were going to drive past and not to be surprised if we got pulled over by the IDF (Israeli Defence Force).

As it happens we drove right alongside the perimeter of the listening station but didn't see sight or sound of the IDF. In fact didn't see another vehicle on the entire journey but that was probably because we were on a red route. We drove up an adjacent hill and S pulled over again at the top. He got his briefcase from the back seat and retrieved a pad, pencil and a pair of binoculars. He explained that the Israelis current strategy was to set up encampments on the edge of the border at various locations but then liked to move on after a few days.

It was designed to keep the entire force mobilised and ready for action as well as to keep the enemy guessing. The hill we were on gave us a great view of the Syrian border in both directions and our job was to record which units were in which locations.

The Israelis always put a regiment flag up when they set up camp which made it easy to report back who was where. It was of course entirely possible that the Israelis were putting up deliberately misleading flags but that wasn't our concern, we just had to report back what we saw.

Having gathered as much info as we could, including regiment markings, vehicle types and size of tents S informed me we had one more stop. We drove down the other side of the hill towards the border and stopped about 100 yards from a mesh fence the other side of which was Syria. We got out of the Jeep and S was looking at a map that he had pulled from his briefcase.

'We are going to check some intel about an exchange of fire down by the fence. Follow me carefully and we'll get you a couple of souvenirs. Walk behind me as we go towards the fence.'

We walked down towards the fence and there on the ground were a dozen or so spent machine gun shell cases.

'Well that's an affirmative. Grab a handful of those and we'll head back. That's a good days work. Remember to walk behind me.'

When we got back to Jeep something was puzzling me. I got why I would walk behind him going towards the fence (presumably so that anyone the other side only saw a British Army uniform) but why on the way back? I decided to ask him.

'Simple. We were in an old minefield and I had the map. Luckily for us the map is still up to date.'

The bullet shells are now proudly displayed on a door lentil in my front room.

FINN MAEDAN

QUEEN AND COUNTRY

TEN

EAST BERLIN JULY 1986
WAITRESS

Madonna was at No 1 with 'Pappa Don't Preach', David Lynch was causing a stir at the box office with Blue Velvet and Prince Andrew wed Sarah Ferguson.

East Berlin was an amazing place. I sort of knew the history surrounding the division of Berlin following WW2 where it had been shared by the allies only for Russia to wall off the area it was responsible for, but I hadn't realised what that really meant. It was pretty much a prison camp full of inmates that had done nothing wrong - the classic wrong place, wrong time situation.

The stereotypes of it being a grey place with grey buildings and even people with grey faces were actually truer than you'd imagine.

There was a distinct general lack of colour partly due to the lack of shops and partly due to their being virtually no advertising anywhere. The only banners or posters you saw were party political messages and there was only one party - the Communists.

We had arrived in Autumn and the grey weather only added to the overall theme and there was an incredible sense of sadness with people almost resigned to the life they had.

A common sight on the way to the office every morning was a long queue to the bakers, one of the few thriving shops, where people would just stand in an orderly line for literally hours just to get their allocation of one loaf per person.

The other feeling you got in East Berlin was that someone was watching you, although that was probably because they were. The place had a definite edge to it, bordering on hostile and we had been instructed never to go anywhere alone and to use different routes as much as possible. The East Berliners were not allowed to talk to westerners unless for official reasons and worse were encouraged to report each other, even their own family, to the Stasi (East German Secret Police) if they witnessed any wrong doing.

I remember walking down the street one evening with R, J and M desperately trying to find a bar when we saw a commotion about 100 yards ahead. A large group of men and women were three deep trying to get a look into the window of a huge Selfridges sized department store that had probably been grand in its day before Russian occupation. There was a genuine buzz about these people which was great to see, so of course we had to find out what the fuss was about.

We eventually bustled our way to the front to see what everyone else was staring at.

It was jam.

The window was dressed with about 30 pots of jam. The jars were perfectly spaced and in little pyramids of three jars. The shop had clearly been proud to display its rich booty. One Berliner caught me speaking to R and turned to us with a huge smile on his face and said excitedly and in English;

'They have jam!'

At the time I just thought he was a nutter but looking back that tells me a lot about human spirit and how much we take for granted.

Following our jam experience and still on the hunt for a bar we noticed a small place with its lights on that appeared to have a few customers in it across the square. We walked in to be greeted by a pretty young German girl who showed us to a table for four. It was a little bright in there for my taste but we didn't care because we could see people eating and drinking wine, and in any case it was cold outside.

J knew some German and remarked to her that he hadn't seen this place before only for her to reply in pretty good English that it had only opened yesterday evening. We ordered four beers only for her to apologise apologised explaining that they only had wine. J showing off now with his German, asked for a wine list. The girl laughed as she went back to the bar. She came back with the label from an empty bottle, handed it to J and said in English;

'Your wine list sir' as she curtsied.

'Four of those then' he smiled back.

'Four?'

'Yep four – we're all thirsty. And can we have the menu please.'

She came back with a tray carrying four bottles of Reisling, four glasses and four menus. The menus were just folded bits of card that had 'Menu' on the front and then one line of German inside. J was pissing himself as he read the menu, the rest of us waiting to hear what it said.

'It says special of the day - sausage and dumplings.'

'What else?'

'That's it.'

Yep the menu had one item on it and now I looked, everyone else was eating sausage and dumplings and drinking the same wine as us.

After another round of four bottles of wine we were well on our merry way and J had built a rapport with our young waitress. It turned out her name was Bettina, she was 22 and a student working evenings. She had been the only remotely friendly East German we'd met so we were milking every opportunity to chat to her.

After another wine round we were the last people in there and whilst Bettina was happy to chat, (she'd pulled up a chair by now), the chef had shut the kitchen up and was standing next to the barman behind the bar both with their arms folded. I'm no scientist when it comes to body language but it was clear these two were fed up and waiting for us to leave.

We were extremely pissed by now but knew we had outstayed our welcome and still aware enough to know you don't cause trouble in East Germany so asked Bettina to get the bill. She returned with the bill and left it with us and went back to join her colleagues. It hit me that until that point we hadn't seen any prices nor asked for them.

The bill showed four meals and twelve bottles of wine. The grand total was 100 East Marks which with the rate we were buying East Marks at, converted to a massive £2.50 each. Surprised at how cheap it was J asked Bettina in German whether there had been a mistake to which she replied that there wasn't. We all pulled out wedges of East Marks and paid £15 each, not because we were trying to be flash but just because the price was so crazily low. Bettina had a 300% tip.

A couple of nights later we decided to go back to that restaurant for a drink. There was no sign of Bettina so J asked the barman where she was. He replied in German.

Apparently she hadn't turned up for work since the night we gave her the big tip.

FINN MAEDAN

QUEEN AND COUNTRY

ELEVEN

EAST BERLIN JULY 1986
CHECKPOINT CHARLIE

Checkpoint Charlie was one of the most famous landmarks in East Berlin. It was originally the third or 'C' opening in the wall that allowed the crossing from East to West if you had the right paperwork. As restaurants and bars were notoriously unreliable in the East, not to mention shops, all embassy personnel were given passes that allowed them free passage to West Berlin.

On the west side of the Charlie crossing there was a fantastic little museum dedicated to the various escape attempts over the years. The stories were heart rendering as most failed and were shot on sight but at the same time testament to man's invention. There were some astonishing attempts including a hang glider from the roof of the tallest building, a homemade (yes homemade!) Submarine, a truck with a fake petrol tank that a man could squeeze into and my personal favourite, a sawn down cabriolet that was precisely half an inch lower than the road barrier it drove straight under.

Because of our diplomatic grades we were entitled to a Red Auschweiss which was effectively a VIP pass. We used Charlie on a daily basis and were used to the routine. As we approached an East German border guard would step out, point his rifle towards us and signal for ID. They always seemed shocked when the Red Auschweiss came out but to be fair without fail they would drop their weapon to their side and salute as we walked past. They must have absolutely hated it.

One night after a few beers M who was from Liverpool and a bit of a scally on the quiet decided that we were going to have a bit of fun with the border guards. The words 'fun' and 'border guard' should never be used in the same sentence.

The following evening after we finished work he said to meet him in the hotel bar as he had something for us. When we got to the bar he got a round in and then another.

'Where are we eating tonight' asked J

'Anywhere as long as its west side' replied M

'Why west side?'

'Because tonight I want to go through

Charlie. I wanna see those Eastie wankers faces.' With that he handed me a jockeys outfit and J a ballet dress. He had a netball top and skirt.

'You must be fucking joking.' Said a shocked J.

'Where did you get this stuff?' Was all I could say.

'Got it off the birds in the Embassy didn't I' he said as he started getting his netball gear on.

Two beers later we were on our way to Checkpoint Charlie. I don't think I'll ever forget the look on the border guards face that day, it was a strange mix of absolute hate and total despair as he had to stand and salute three idiots dressed as a ballerina, a jockey and a netball player walking past waving a Red Auschweiss and just to rub it in singing our favourite rugby song

'A-ru-ti-ta. A-ru-ti-ta. A-ru-ti-ta-ta,'

The next day we were summoned to see the Head of Chancery. He showed us into the Strong Room and was clearly not happy.

'I know all about your stupid antics last night.'

Shit, word travels fast I thought. We stood there not saying a word.

'Life out here is hard enough for Embassy staff and the Red Auschweiss is a privilege allowed us by the East German authorities that is essential to the well-being and morale of my people.'

We were all looking at our feet.

'My counterpart in the East German government has said he had a good mind to make a formal complaint to Whitehall. I had to apologise profusely, which believe me I am not comfortable with, or happy about.'

J broke the silence. 'I won't insult you by trying to excuse our actions and can only say that we are sorry for any embarrassment we have caused you.'

The Head of Chancery looked all three of us up and down.

'We will leave it there but make sure I do not hear about any more incidents.'

We turned to leave.

'One last thing.'

We paused.

'I discussed this with the Ambassador who was quietly amused. Anything that pisses those Stasi bastards off is fine with us. But of course I never said that.'

All in all not my finest hour.

FINN MAEDAN

QUEEN AND COUNTRY

TWELVE

HANOI MARCH 1987
M.I.A.

Boy George was at No 1 with 'Everything I Own', The Untouchables was a hit at the cinema and a car ferry disaster in the port of Zeebrugge claimed many lives.

Going to Hanoi was like stepping back into time. It was 1987 which was only 12 years after the war with the US and there were plenty of reminders around. It started as the plane came in to land at Hanoi Airport, where although the runway had been re-laid, all around it were craters left from the severe bombing it once endured. I was working with K who I really liked and was always good fun to be around, one of those blokes who always seemed happy. The primary objective of our trip was to install a new Intruder Detection system but because the Americans still hadn't opened an Embassy there yet we had a couple of far more interesting jobs to do for them.

Waiting for us outside the airport was a London black cab. Admittedly nothing special if you land at Heathrow but in the jungle of Vietnam it was a surreal sight especially as Hanoi had very few cars and the largest bicycle population in the world. The Ambassador, who was a colourful character to say the least, had forgone the usual Bentley/Rolls status symbol and instead insisted on something overtly English. It actually worked well as the locals loved to see it and it often brought smiles to the faces of children. The route from the airport to the Embassy had more reminders of recent times, as every now and then there was a US tank or other armored vehicle in a ditch beside the road. They were mostly just rusting shells now as the locals had stripped anything sellable from the once mighty war machines but even the carcasses left behind were a formidable sight.

On arrival at the embassy we went through the usual procedure of unpacking. Other than what we were carrying, the kit had been sent out previously and was waiting at the Embassy in sealed boxes. Our first job was to check the boxes hadn't been tampered with and to confirm it was all there. A quick telegram back to The Park followed to say we were ready to start the next day. Before going to check in at our hotel we were to meet with the onsite MI6 operative to for a briefing as to the US requirements. He explained the work we did for the US and the current political situation as well as briefing us on a reconnaissance trip to a couple of local villages we were going on the following day.

After the meeting we decided to call it a day and went to the hotel for a couple of beers and an early night. The hotel was one of the worst I've ever stayed in. It was like a military hospital with long corridors off of which were small rooms with hard tiled floors and bizarre doors with opaque glass panels that you couldn't quite see in but could make out body shapes. Just to cap it off there was a sink but no water, a toilet that didn't flush and when you flicked the light on hundreds of cockroaches scattered into their hidey holes waiting for the light to go off again so that they could come out. It was the best excuse I've ever had for maximising time in the bar and minimising time in this room.

The Vietnam conflict was (and still is some 40 years later) a political hot potato in the US and as they refused to have a presence there the Brits coordinated by MI6 looked after their interests from the mundane   stuff like visa's, travelers in difficulty etc. to intelligence gathering for the CIA. One of the most sensitive issues that remained was the question of MIA's, those men that were missing in action and so far not accounted for. Whilst everyone understands how awful it must be for the families of these men to not know and therefore not grieve properly, there was huge disagreement between governments as to their whereabouts. A significant number would have been killed and the bodies simply not recovered but it was the others that were the center of dispute.

MI6 had plenty of evidence, mostly anecdotal but some actual of desertions, particularly into Laos, Thailand and Cambodia, but with veteran support as strong as it was at that time in the US and with an incredible number of votes at play, the US government daren't deny the idea that they were all held in bamboo cells by local villages and used as forced labour. It had long been thought that films like Rambo were commissioned by the CIA as effective pro military, anti-communist propaganda.

There were regular stories in the US press regarding 'sightings' often with aerial photos of numbers carved out in paddy fields or sticks laid out to form a coded message. These stories made great headlines but the question remained as to whether there was there any substance behind them. As the USA's strongest ally in Vietnam, the UK supported the efforts to investigate these 'sightings' but were quietly skeptical about the whole thing.

We knew that the Vietnamese government desperately wanted to open trade links with the US and had no interest whatsoever in holding ageing soldiers as prisoners. Apart from anything else with 12 years now passed, for the soldiers to remain healthy and effective labour they would have to be fed well which most villages could ill afford. MI6 believed that the vast majority of MIA's were just scared young men who escaped the war any way they could and were now running bars somewhere on the Thai coast. Nevertheless, we were happy to do what we could to help the CIA's investigations.

In the morning, the MI6 guy met us at the hotel in the Embassy Jeep. With him he had one of the local staff who had come along as a guide and interpreter. He said we were going out to a couple of remote villages where there had supposedly been sightings of POW's. He had one rucksack full of water and another bag containing sweets and pens which he said were the most effective currency when trading for information in the villages.

Riding in an open top Jeep, firstly through the streets of Hanoi and then down dirt tracks and through paddy fields towards villages was a truly amazing experience and sadly at 23 I had no idea how lucky I was to be experiencing these insights into another culture.

We were driving along a sort of raised bank

between two paddy fields when we could see the mass of wooden huts and tents ahead which was the village we were heading for. The interpreter knew this village and said he had a friend who was a farmer there but reminded us that we were not to stray from the well-worn paths as the jungle was still riddled with mines and unexploded shells. On arrival a mass of kids ran out to meet us, some trying to get into the jeep, some jumping up at us but all shouting the two English words they knew, 'dollar' and 'candy'. Our interpreter was trying to shoo them away as me and K handed out sweets and pens. Then we noticed something that got the MI6 guy all excited - one of the kids had white blonde hair.

Obviously that was not a natural hair colour in the region but it wasn't that rare either as plenty of 'collaboration' took place but the majority was found on young teens rather than small kids and this particular 'collaboration' could only have happened about 6 years ago. After some negotiation and a considerable bribe for the village elder, we were taken into the village to meet the kids mum. Our spook buddy was only really interested in the dad and after some persuading she admitted he was indeed American but someone she had met in a bar in Hanoi. After another payment, the elder allowed us a tour of the village with access to all areas, there was certainly no sign of a wasting bearded GI in a bamboo cage as Hollywood would have you believe. We finished the search and drove back to Hanoi.

We will probably never know the full circumstances of the little boy's father but we were sure it did not relate to anything untoward.

QUEEN AND COUNTRY

THIRTEEN

HANOI MARCH 1987
'RUN YOU CUNTS'

There were two odd things about Hanoi. 1, the highest number of foreign nationals in the country were Swedes. 2, the Vietnamese people were not allowed to congregate in groups in public.

These two facts together meant the Swedes, who liked a drink or two, had to find out of town places to go and party. One of their favourite weekends was to drive up into the hills about 2 hours out of Hanoi to an old Dacha now owned by the Swedish Embassy where they would just drink, dance and sing Swedish songs. Myself and K had been invited along and of course jumped at the chance.

K wanted to take photos of a waterfall nearby whereas it was the drinking and rugby songs that sold it to me. What I was about to find out was that the Swedes are mad bastards.

The MI6 guy heard we were going and asked me to get him an invite which I did. The Americans had this theory that some of their MIA's were being used as human mine clearers by the Vietnamese, where they would be stripped and made to walk into the jungle with a long piece of string. If there was an explosion another mine was cleared, if not the string highlighted a safe trail which would be then be mapped. Again the UK intelligence services were highly sceptical of this theory but one of the areas the yanks wanted checking happened to be close by the weekend venue.

We left for the Dacha straight after work on Friday and got there for around 6. The trail was virtually empty all the way there with only the odd farmer walking a donkey to be seen. It was somewhat surreal to go from a trail surrounded by jungle in the middle of nowhere to pull in to a car park full of Swedish Diplomatic plates.

We walked in to a huge open plan hall with a makeshift bar at one end. There were a few people sat around in groups drinking and a huge circle of about 50 blokes beer in hand singing some indecipherable Swedish nonsense. I could see a few sleeping bags that been dumped in various locations presumably where they intended to crash. As soon as the Swedes spotted us, we were beckoned into the circle and handed beers. Whilst we had no idea what they were singing about, the atmosphere was infectious - a high stress life needs a suitable release and this was clearly it.

A few hours later the MI6 guy was out cold half inside a sleeping bag and me and K were well on our way to being pissed. We had started joining in with the Swedish songs and even had them singing our very own a-ru-ti-ta when there was a loud whoompf outside.

One of the Swedes said it was 'just a mine' and that most probably an animal, possibly a warthog, had strayed on to it. He kept saying 'bacon for breakfast' in heavily accented English much to the delight of his Swedish buddies. I looked at K and we clearly thought the same thing. Could this be what the Americans had said was happening?

We convinced two of the Swedes to take us to search for the 'bacon' and we set off down a well-used track with torches. After about ten minutes we saw activity ahead and the two Swedes dropped to a crouch position with their fingers over their mouths. We copied and waited silently. Although it was pitch black the moonlight was glinting on what turned out to be four or five Vietnamese soldiers pushing two clearly naked men.

'Jesus, the yanks were right' whispered K.

'Quiet' said one of the Swedes. 'Follow in

silence, we need to see more.'

'You must be joking' replied K.

'Don't worry we are Special Forces. You be OK if you copy'

Fucking great. Here we were in the middle of the Vietnamese jungle playing soldiers with Swedish SAS. I don't think I'd ever been so far out of my depth and if it wasn't for the beer giving me some form of false bravery I'd have been legging it in the other direction. The lead Swede inched forward staying in the crouch position until we got close enough to see a bit more. It was now obvious the naked guys were not western but oriental, probably Vietnamese.

Then the inevitable happened - one of them spotted us.

Me and K looked at the Swedes for guidance as to what to do next when in an almost comic moment the lead one jumped to his feet and screamed out something in Swedish.

We all ran as fast as we could back the way we came. I was doing all I could to keep up with the Swede when after what felt like ages but was probably only a few minutes had passed, I realised we had lost the other two. Somehow we had also taken the wrong trail and now didn't know where the Dacha was.

We were just running further into the jungle with the sound of Vietnamese shouting somewhere behind us and thankfully getting further away.

About 10 minutes later, the Swede stopped and put his finger to his lip again. We listened intensely not moving a muscle, but it was silent. He whispered that he thought we'd lost them and now we had to find or make shelter as it was too dark to go looking for the Dacha and we were now disoriented. It was then that I knew where the phrase 'fuck this for a game of soldiers' must have originated.

We carried on walking slowly and quietly for another 15 minutes, him using his torch to check the path ahead. Luckily we came across a small clearing with a bamboo and stone hut, probably a farmer's rain shelter. The Swede checked it out and confirmed it was OK for us to use. Although it smelt pretty bad it was dry, which was a good thing because it had just started to rain and when it rained in Vietnam, it really rained. We sat down and the Swede introduced himself as Frond. It was going to be a long night so he started telling me a few war stories and when he ran out of those he started teaching me some Swedish. After a few lessons in the basics relating to beer and women's body parts he moved on to all the swear words. Getting into this language training thing, I asked him what it was he shouted when we were seen.

He started laughing and said; 'I think the literal translation into English would be 'run you cunts'.'

I remember telling him the only famous Swede I could think of was the chef on the Muppets which he laughed at (lucky for me) and he responded with Monty Python gags which were clearly funnier to Europeans than they were to me. I was on my way to becoming an honorary Swede when he got a small round tin out of his jeans pocket. Inside was a black paste that he took a pinch of and shoved under his top lip. He handed the tin to me saying it was used by the Swedish Special Forces to keep them warm and so I had some too. It turned out that it was only chewing tobacco but as a non-smoker it gave me my first (and last) nicotine rush. Within about 5 minutes I was laughing like a halfwit at everything he said, even the Monty Python jokes that he'd already told.

I learnt three things that day. 1. the Vietnamese were using their own dissidents for mine detecting. 2. me and tobacco were never going to be friends and 3. the Swedish for 'Run you cunts.'

FINN MAEDAN

QUEEN AND COUNTRY

FOURTEEN

SANA'A AUGUST 1987
CARGO

Los Lobos were at No 1 with 'La Bamba', Full Metal Jacket was the hit film at the cinema and a gunman killed 14 innocent people in Hungerford.

The Embassy in Sana'a, the capital of North Yemen was moving to new premises. In a pre-trip briefing we heard that 20 tons of equipment for the new building had to be escorted out there and subsequently secured on site. D told the section that it would need a team of three and the job would take about six weeks, in which time the cargo must never leave our sight. He then called out three names for the job. One was mine.

I was told that it would be very hot in Sana'a and whilst power had been confirmed as available in the new building, the air conditioning would not be up and running during our time there. On the plus side there would be no diplomatic staff around as they would be working in the old building until the new one was ready to handover, although we should still wear a suit while representing OSD in transit and to and from the building each day.

The three that were assigned to the job, me, M and K then went to a separate meeting to get the travel details. It became clear this was a one off job and due to the amount of kit being transported, the FCO had commissioned a cargo plane for the journey out.

Our role was to watch the crates loaded on to a convoy of trucks at The Park and once sealed ride with the trucks to Stansted Airport where we would oversee the transfer to the plane. Once the plane landed in Sana'a we were to supervise its unloading, clear it through the airport and escort it to the new building which we then had to secure.

The first part of the trip had gone well. All of the kit was now in sealed wooden crates with 'HBM Diplomatic Service' emblazoned all over them and was safely in the Park trucks. We were in a big blue convoy on our way down the motorway.

On arrival at Stansted we were guided towards a hangar slightly away from the main terminal where we pulled up alongside a huge aircraft the likes of I'd never seen before. The driver told me it was a 'Guppy' which was sort of a cut down Hercules and the tail end was at right angles to the main fuselage opening up the body for loading. It looked like the Dover ferry from behind and was that huge that you could have driven the articulated trucks straight on.

That however wasn't the plan because this was a one way trip only and the trucks were staying in the UK so the crates were loaded off the trucks and on to the plane. After a couple of hours the plane's tail end was locked back into place.

As was standard procedure, the Park drivers would wait on the tarmac until we were airborne. We used the opportunity to grab a quick coffee and went looking for the small hangar waiting room.

We were helping ourselves to coffee from a vending machine when three guys in dirty orange boiler suits walked in. To my shock they introduced themselves as the crew.

'So you three are the spooks dropping the kit off then. It's all on board so you can go back to bed now.'

'Yeah funny. What time do we leave?'

'What do you mean we? You don't think you're coming do you?' He wasn't joking.

K was getting agitated now. 'Are you taking the piss? We are escorting this equipment all the way to Sana'a'.

'Well I'm the Captain and no one told me I

had passengers. There are four seats up front and three crew flying so unless you lot want to fly the fucking thing you aren't coming.'

'I suggest you call your bosses and I will do the same.' said a now angry K.

K called The Park emergency line and eventually spoke to a senior officer who said to sit tight as it would have to be referred to Whitehall. It was a disaster. Clearly there had been a breakdown in communication and now the kit had been loaded on to a cargo plane and it turned out that no one had checked about arrangements for the escorts.

An hour later the captain came back in with three boiler suits.

'Right. Apparently we have to take you. You can be strapped to a bench for 11 hours or strapped on top of a crate where you might get some sleep. I say might because the idiots who have insisted on this don't realise the aircraft hold is not heated and if that doesn't kill you the noise from the four prop engines will deafen you as there is no noise muffling. I suggest you change into these boiler suits as the cargo area is filthy and these are the only warmth you're going to get.' He held out three filthy sleeping bags.

We couldn't believe what we were hearing. K called The Park back and had it confirmed. If we didn't fly today it could be weeks before it was all arranged again and they couldn't afford that as the new building was lying unprotected. Like it or not we were going.

Now in dirty boiler suits, the Captain gave us our allotted sleeping bag and a pair of ear defenders. He reminded us there was no toilet on board and sarcastically pointed out that the stewardess had the night off. K took a bench seat which we nicknamed 'economy' and M and I opted for the 'crate class' experience. Using heavy crate straps the crew tied us to our respective crates in case of turbulence and told us to get the ear defenders on before the engines started up. The Captain inspected our straps and handed us a 1 liter bottle of lemonade each which he said was all he had. Now more concerned than angry he said;

'It's all I've got I'm afraid but you'll need something if you get thirsty. It's going to get very cold back here so once we are over the ocean I will drop as low as I can. Any higher than 5000 feet and I've got three bodies to deal with. We may be giving a few boats a fright. The cockpit is heated so you can take it in turns to come up front and warm up.'

About an hour into the flight I realised what he was talking about. The noise of the four prop engines was deafening even with the ear defenders on and I was so cold I was uncontrollably shivering.

I couldn't see the others but imagined they were the same. Somehow, probably my body shutting down, I fell asleep. I'm not sure how long I slept but I woke feeling thirsty. I reached for the lemonade only to find it was frozen solid. I didn't have any gloves on and my fingers were tingling - I don't think I'd ever been so cold.

I decided to go up front to warm up and passed M on the way. We couldn't talk because of the noise but he was smiling and I guessed had already been up front as he was in good spirits and didn't seem to be shivering. He was pointing at his frozen lemonade and I gave him the thumbs up to indicate mine was the same.

The cockpit was surprisingly cramped for such a huge aircraft but it was warm and it felt so good to be out of the freezing hold. The noise level was also better and the Captain handed me a headset so I could speak to the crew.

'You boys are either nutters, stupid or both. I wouldn't sit back there for all the money in China.'

I was going to correct him 'you meant tea' but was too cold to be bothered. I just wanted to get warm.

'Look out there' He pointed out of his window and I could see that we were virtually skimming the ocean.

'Cool huh? I don't think we've ever flown this low over the sea before eh boys? Made the trip quite exciting really.' I was pleased for him.

He handed over a bottle of Whiskey and

told me it would be the quickest way to get warm. I took a long swig. He wasn't wrong. After about 20 minutes having warmed up nicely I went back to my crate and strapped myself back in pulling the sleeping bag right over my head. The whiskey must have done its job as the next thing I remember was waking up as we were landing at Sana'a International Airport.

It was a relief to be on firm ground and a stark contrast to feel the dry hot air and bright sunshine as they opened the cockpit door. The next good news came from the Captain. He told us that Sana'a wasn't equipped for the height of the aircraft and so had no stairs that would reach. In addition because customs hadn't cleared us yet we couldn't open the rear freight doors to drop the ramp.

There was nothing else for it, we had to throw the emergency rope down from the cockpit door to the ground and shimmy down it. I always thought the locals in their comfortable flowing Arab outfits must have blinked and looked twice at three European idiots climbing down a 40ft rope in full business suits. The trip was getting better and better.

We were met by a couple of Yemeni officials in full military dress who were accompanied by about half a dozen soldiers. The guy who appeared to be in charge spoke pretty good English and told us we needed to go and wait in the customs hanger where our equipment would be loaded into. K tried to tell him that we had to stay with the equipment and he said that there was no shelter by the aircraft and we wouldn't last long in this heat. If you ask me he was making a lot of sense and I was hoping K would back down. Eventually a compromise was reached whereby we would go to the hangar but only if it had full view of the aircraft and the freight access would not open without K's permission.

Somewhat relieved I walked over to the hangar, which was an oven its own right but at least shaded from the direct sun. I noticed that there was a white chalk line down the middle of the hangar and a single chair on one side with nothing on the other. There were armed guards front and back presumably for our benefit to protect the cargo.

Eventually the Customs Chief, who was the brother of the guy who had met us previously, turned up and gave the go ahead to unload. The Embassy had lined up three locally hired trucks that were waiting the other side of the hangar and ready to be loaded once all crates were cleared by the Yemeni's.

We arranged for the hired labour to be allowed through and they started to offload the aircraft. We decided the three of us could maintain 'eyes on' by placing ourselves at the back of the plane, at the entrance to the hangar and in the hangar supervising where the crates were put. I was in the hangar when the first crate was brought in and placed on the floor. Almost immediately one of the soldiers came over and motioned that the crate had to be moved to the other side of the white line. It seemed the side with the chair in was not ours to use.

It was of no consequence to me and it's difficult to argue with an agitated Yemini holding a Kalashnikov so we carried on as instructed, taking it in turns to be out in the heat until the last crate went into the hangar. The two Yemeni brothers, now nicknamed by us as Bill and Ben, came in and asked to speak to an Embassy representative. One of the Ambassador's aides was waiting with the trucks outside and came in with an Embassy interpreter.

After what seemed a rather heated exchange the aide explained to us that a 'clearance fee' was needed to get the kit through customs and the Clearance Officer was their cousin. Essentially a bribe was needed to clear customs, which was we knew was standard practice in Yemen but because of the amount of freight the size of the bribe was higher than the aide was able to agree. He told us he would have to call London and it was now 10 PM their time.

It was pretty obvious we wouldn't be out

of there anytime soon and clearly Bill had the same opinion as to be fair had organised for some very welcome water and bread to keep us going.

We were sat on crates washing the bread down with the water when a fat guy in a suit walked into the hangar and sat on the chair opposite our freight.

'I'm sorry sir you can't stay here.' Pointed out K.

Bill interjected. 'Actually he can. The gentleman is a representative of the Russian Embassy and that half of the hangar is their customs clearance area.'

A small brown parcel was placed next to the Russian who proceeded to light a cheap cigarette.

'You have to be fucking joking'

'No joke sir. He can stay until his parcel is cleared. Just like you'

Bill and Ben were both smiling. Very clever.

The old Ruskis had heard about our equipment coming and this was their way of being on hand to witness events. None of this was shaping up as planned and I had a feeling that there was more to come. I wasn't wrong.

A group of soldiers came running in, stood in a line and pointed their weapons at us. The leader said something in Arabic to Ben, who turned to us and said;

'We have been alerted to a possible

shipment of illegal goods and therefore you have to open some of your crates.'

'Not a chance mate. This is clearly labeled Diplomatic Baggage and therefore we do not have to open it whatever your alerts are - as you well know.'

'You are not leaving until some of the crates have been opened.'

'Fine, we'll stay here while you rack up an almighty diplomatic incident.'

Ben walked over to the Russian and whispered something in his ear. He came back to us and said;

'Perhaps if we point out three crates to be opened we could leave it at that and you can go.'

'What the three crates fat boy has just told you to ask for? Piss off.'

We told the Ambassador's aide to inform the Ambassador and get word to Whitehall that there was a standoff. K asked to use a telephone so that he could call The Park.

A few minutes later, K came back saying that subject to anything Whitehall might come back with, under no circumstances were we to open any of the crates. Furthermore if necessary we would load up the plane and go back. After a very hot and tense hour, with the smell of cheap cigarettes starting to make me gag, the Ambassador's aide returned.

He called us into the corner and said he had been given instructions from Whitehall.

Turning back was not an option as the plane had to leave in less than an hour and did not have enough fuel for the load in any case. Having said that, the Yemeni's didn't know this so for the time being we could still use that option as leverage.

He also said that as a last resort MI6 had given permission for three crates of unclassified equipment to be opened in the event a compromise was needed but under no circumstances should classified equipment be exposed to the Russians.

'Fucking brilliant between a rock and a hard place.' Said K.

Then K came up with a great idea. We were going to suggest a compromise of opening three crates but we got three 'exempts' to use. We would just have to hope that if we used our three 'exempts' they picked unclassified crates. K put the compromise to Ben who had another conflab with the Russian.

'By the way I will be letting the Yemeni authorities know that you are letting fat boy here run the show.'

'Firstly we accept your offer and secondly I was simply suggesting to him that it might get noisy when we open a couple of your crates and therefore he might want to leave. As it happens he declined.'

'Yeah funny that'

For the next 30 minutes you could have cut

the tension in the air with a knife. We had labeled each crate with a OSD ref number and K had the corresponding sheet in his pocket. The sheet was never explicit in case it got lost but it had a series of numbers and letters that told him what was in each crate - or so we hoped.

They picked the largest crate they could see. K checked his list and nodded. The soldiers jumped on top and prised it open with crowbars. They started looking through the contents and both Bill & Ben went to inspect. We knew it was nothing classified, just spare parts for an emergency generator.

Ben nodded at the Russian and he nodded back. The second crate they picked drew a quick response of 'Exempt' from K. He knew exactly what was in that one. They honored this and picked another crate which K agreed to. They were mightily disappointed when they found hundreds of plugs, sockets and light fittings. For their third pick they had noticed M deliberately stand in front of a suitcase sized box. Assuming he was trying to conceal it they insisted it be opened. K used his second exempt. They said it had to be that one as he had already used his exempt.

'But we had three exempts'

'You must be mistaken we only agreed one. That box must be opened.'

'No chance. If you open this you are in breach of every diplomatic protocol and your

Ambassador in London will not be too happy when his Embassy gets a visit tomorrow.' This clearly rattled Bill who was now chatting away in Arabic to Ben and the Russian. We could actually hear the Russian now as his voice was getting angrier and he was virtually shouting at them in Arabic.

'I'm sorry but we insist' said Ben. The soldiers pushed past us and took the box.

'You'll regret this' K was warning.

Using a knife, they opened the outer box carefully and pulled out another box this time a red plastic one with 'Hilti' written on the side. They opened it to find what looked like an industrial drill. They passed it between each other making sure the Russian got a good view and then said it would have to be confiscated.

'You've gone way too far now. Your action constitutes the unwarranted theft of Her Majesty's Diplomatic Freight.'

'Nevertheless we have to confiscate this for further inspection as it exactly matches the description of the illegal freight we were alerted about.'

'Fine. You'll be the ones in the shit. Now let us get on our way.'

Ben nodded and the soldiers withdrew. They opened up the big hangar doors at the back and the Ambassador's aide came in with a swarm of locals who started to load up the equipment onto waiting trucks.

Personally I had mixed feelings, partly of relief that we were getting out of there but also a sense of defeat that we had just lost a Diplomatic bag. The truth was that we had no choice but whatever the circumstances it would surely be a blot on our various careers. K explained to the Ambassador's aide what had happened as we got on the truck and headed for the new Embassy building. I decided to break the silence.

'What did they get then?' K looked at me, paused and said;

'A drill'

'I know what it looked like, but what was it?'

He burst out laughing. 'Like I said. A drill'

'But I thought..'

'Yeah so did those stupid fuckers. I made a meal of it so that they thought they had something. The good stuff is safe and sound in the back.'

That was probably the best double bluff I've ever seen.

QUEEN AND COUNTRY

FIFTEEN

SANA'A AUGUST 1987
BLOODY GOOD ROAST

It was Saturday and after a day's slog in the non-air-conditioned new building, it was a nice surprise and great relief to us to find that the small bar at the bottom of our hotel sold beer. It was surprise because Yemen was a dry country and we had been told there was nowhere you could get a beer. The drug of choice in the region was something called Qat, a naturally grown leaf that the Yemenis packed into their cheek letting the natural narcotic seep into their blood stream giving them a high. We saw loads of guys walking around with one cheek distorted by a huge lump and at first thought it was some kind or horrible deforming disease until we were told about the Qat by a taxi driver, who incidentally also had a cheek full.

The beer was only cocktail size cans of Heineken, the sort you get these days on EasyJet, but it was cold and it was beer. It wasn't cheap, about three times the UK price but we weren't going to bother about that. We reckoned the bar owner had some dodgy deal going on with one of the airlines.

Having polished off about eight of these, which was probably only a pint in any case, I noticed that a young Arab was sat on his own also drinking a Heineken. M raised his can to him in a cheers motion.

The young Arab came over and introduced himself as Prince Abdullah and started chatting to us in very good English. After the experience at the airport, we were on heightened alert and careful not to give anything away as to the purpose of our visit. We came up with some nonsense about being electricians working on the new building. To be fair he didn't seem that interested in what we were doing and just wanted to talk about football and his beloved Liverpool. We had doubts he was a real Prince but he seemed a genuinely nice guy and explained that this was a 'special' bar that the hotel was allowed to run for expats only although royals and the police would unofficially frequent it. He then asked if we would miss our 'Sunday Roast' which was an odd question to be asked in a semi-legal bar in the middle of Yemen. He went on to tell us that his uncle had been a chef to the British Army stationed in Aden and his family were all told how the British had to have a roast every Sunday with his uncle acclaimed as the best roast chef in Aden. Abdullah, full of pride for his uncle's reputation, insisted we join him the following day for a Sunday roast at the restaurant he was now working at. It was all a bit surreal but we politely agreed saying how great that would be thinking it was the Heineken talking and there was no way he would turn up in any case.

The next day we checked the foyer of the hotel at 12 just in case he turned up. There was no one there as we expected and we started to walk into town for something to do when a white limousine pulled up alongside us that had what looked like Stag antlers fixed to the front grill. A blacked out window went down to reveal the smiling face of Prince Abdulah.

'Sorry I'm late guys, get in, my uncle is honoured to be preparing Sunday roast again.' We couldn't really refuse. We still didn't know if he really was a Prince but he certainly had an impressive car. We drove for about 10 minutes along the only main road in Sana'a towards the town center when we felt a judder as it turned off the road onto a dirt track. The smooth ride had just got very bumpy when we slowed down at what looked like a ramshackle old sentry box. A little old man wearing what looked like a big nappy and carrying an old WW2 Lee Enfield rifle came out to speak to the driver. Following an exchange of Arabic he jumped to attention and saluted. It was like a scene out of Dad's Army.

Another five minutes and we pulled up outside a row of sand coloured portacabin huts. We all got out and Abdullah greeted the man waiting for us. Abdullah introduced his uncle and said he couldn't stay as he was busy but would send a car in two hours. We were in the middle of the desert and had no idea where we were so didn't want to think about that car not coming back.

The uncle spoke perfect English and seemed very happy to have a couple of Brit punters. He showed us into one of the portacabins that had been laid out like a cafe with around 15 tables all covered in red check plastic table cloths. There was no one else in there so we picked a table with our backs to the wall facing the door. It was a sparse room with a serving hatch onto a kitchen and three pictures on the wall, all of Yasser Arafat, the leader of the outlawed Palestinian Liberation Organisation (PLO) in various poses. The uncle came out with homemade lemonade and said he would be back in fifteen minutes with a lamb roast. It was a weird situation but following the journey nothing much came as a surprise. A few guys came in and took a table followed by a few more. Some were in full Arab regalia others in green khakis but all were wearing, black and white checked headgear matching that of Yasser Arafat. None of them seemed to notice us but we were starting to get a little nervous. The uncle appeared with two plates of what has to be said was a great attempt at a Sunday roast. The veg wasn't quite what we are used to but tasty nonetheless, we daren't ask what animal the meat originated from but the roast potatoes were excellent. Maybe because of the lack of decent food so far, or maybe just due to the surrealness of the whole situation, it felt like it was the best roast I'd ever had.

The place got even busier and there were people waiting outside for an available table when the uncle came to tell us that the car had arrived for us. He wouldn't take any money, saying this had honoured his family name. We had been fed well by people who had been nothing but friendly, paid nothing for it and still it was a relief to be heading back to the hotel.

The next day we were telling one of the Embassy staff about this amazing but odd restaurant we found when he laughed.

'Were there by any chance pictures of Arafat on the walls?'

'Actually yes why?'

'You dicks, you went for Sunday dinner on

a PLO training camp.'

'Shit.'

'Shit is right. I don't know what's worse, the fact that the yanks periodically blow the shit out of those camps or what the Ambassador would say if he knew you two idiots were sitting down for a nice cosy lunch with a bunch of terrorists.'

There wasn't much we could say to that, but it was a bloody good roast.

FINN MAEDAN

QUEEN AND COUNTRY

SIXTEEN

THE US YEARS 1988 - 1990
BOSTON

Phil Collins was at No 1 with 'Groovy kind of Love', Die Hard was breaking box office records and Ben Johnson had been stripped of Olympic Gold following a positive drugs test.

It was a real buzz to be selected for a full posting to Washington. It was regarded as the best posting you could get and usually reserved for high fliers, in my view not something you would regard me as.

It took around a year to do all the training courses, the down side of which was that there would be no short trips during the period, but obviously worth it for three years state-side.

Once arrived and settled in I was added to the plan for what we called maintenance visits to the US outstations. We looked after Bermuda, Bahamas, Jamaica, Belize and all the British Consulates dotted around the US.

To ease me in gently my first trip was to the Consulate in Boston which in US terms was just up the road. It was looking like being an interesting one as intelligence was coming through that the area was an IRA hub and breeding ground for young operatives who could fly in and out from Ireland with ease. We knew that the main source of the IRA's funding was from the US and the Irish Northern Aid Committee (NorAid) were a self-proclaimed fund raising organisation that had a huge presence in Boston. It was NorAid who were believed to be, by both the UK and US governments, the source of much of the fund raising.

We had thought for some time that there had been attempts at espionage attacks on the Consulate and although there had been some strange happenings nothing had ever been proven.

A few weeks earlier one of the Consulate registry staff had reported something interesting. She claimed that having locked up in the usual way on a Friday evening, when she came in on Monday three cabinets had the wrong locking styles on them. In her view the cabinets had been opened and the styles replaced in a hurry on the wrong cabinets. I was asked to take a look and see if I could find any evidence of lock tampering.

I had some equipment with me in one diplomatic bag and when taking only one bag, rather than drivers at the tarmac and all that rigmarole we would simply purchase a second seat for the bag and strap it in next to us for the flight. That way we would travel as normal passengers.

I booked two seats and arrived at Dulles Airport with just hand luggage and the dip bag. I went to the security area and they were well versed in handling dip bags and had procedures to deal with them. They knew it couldn't be opened and couldn't go through the x-ray machine so the procedure was for a supervisor to be called who would I would pass the bag to behind the x-ray machine while my hand luggage went through as normal. The supervisor would hand it back after I had passed through the metal detector. On this occasion I handed the bag to the supervisor who gave me a lined notebook to sign. It had a page dedicated to my flight number and about eleven signatures already in place.

'That's a lot of diplomats on one flight' I pointed out.

The supervisor looked puzzled and replied;

'No, you're the only one today so far sir.'

'But what about the other 11 signatures?'

'Oh - they're not diplomats; we use the same book for registered gun carriers.'

It was that moment it hit me I was living and working in the good old US of A.

Boston was a very cosmopolitan city with 30's architecture and friendly people. In the Consulate I met with the lady who had reported the 'event' and she showed me what had happened. There were three four drawer filing cabinets where they kept sensitive information. Each cabinet was secured with a locking bar that ran through each drawer handle, attached top and bottom and then locked in place with a mechanical combination lock, the sort you see on a bank safe.

Because she was convinced there was foul play she had colour coded the locking bars with small discrete stickers and applied the same to the cabinets. She told me that the previous Monday all cabinets had the wrong locking bar secured in place.

I spent the day stripping the locks down individually to their hundreds of component parts and inspecting them for tampering. I didn't find anything suspicious and refitted the locks. The one thing I thought odd was that when asked she didn't really know the order, left to right, of the colours she used. In fact she thought that irrelevant as it was all about the colour on the locking bar matching the sticker on the cabinet. That led me to conclude that the real issue here was that someone was moving the stickers to wind her up. Now whether that was a mischievous colleague or the IRA playing mind games I will never know. Either way, no complaints from me as it got me a nice little trip to Boston.

QUEEN AND COUNTRY

SEVENTEEN

THE US YEARS 1988 - 1990
ASSISTANCE REQUIRED

Kylie & Jason were at No 1 with 'Especially for You', Batman was the must see film and dozens were killed when a Boeing 737 hit the M1 Motorway in the Est Midlands.

My boss took a call one day from his counterpart at a friendly Embassy (probably best not to name them here) a little way down Massachusetts Avenue.

A crisis had broken out on one of their borders and artillery fire had been exchanged by both sides. As a consequence their world-wide communication traffic had gone through the roof and as luck would have it their cypher equipment had broken down meaning they were unable to convert classified communications.

We knew what equipment they had and we

also knew it was pretty old. We certainly didn't carry any spares and weren't sure if they did either. My boss said we would be happy to help and asked me to go down that morning after we'd cleared it with the MI6 head of Station.

I went to see the MI6 guy and he called one of his team in. They discussed the situation and decided this was a great opportunity to gather some intelligence they needed. They asked me to go and look at the problem and make sure that if I got the equipment going to stay there while the information came through. In addition they needed to know the location and type of every sensor and lock on the route to the Strong room. The guys were already confident they could get into the building but there wasn't enough detail on where the catch points were. With that information they could get in and out in a couple of hours.

When I arrived the local team couldn't have been friendlier, we were their last hope in a crisis and any concerns about security, especially with 'friends' had gone out of the window.

I have no idea what grade the person was that met me but he clearly had access to the heart of their operation and showed me to the cypher gear. They had a single combination lock Strong Room which was behind two other secured corridor doors. Each door had a sensor on it and there were four ceiling mounted infra-red detectors, two in the corridor, one at the entrance hall and one just outside the Strong Room.

Inside, there were about half a dozen guys standing around a small table at the back of the room next to a teleprinter that was silent due to no traffic coming through. The guys were clearly panicking because they couldn't communicate with home on what was becoming a very sensitive situation.

Worse, while the UK had publicly taken their side on the incident the US had remained quiet and could go either way. As a result they could not afford to let the traffic come in unencrypted.

I recognised the kit straight away and our records weren't wrong, it was about the oldest cypher gear still in active service. On the one hand this was good because it wasn't a particularly complex bit of kit but I hadn't ever worked on a real life one of these, I'd only seen one on a training course.

I took the casing off and luckily for me I realised what the issue was straight away. This particular piece of kit was designed to work in the field and therefore was connected to a large brown wooden box that had two car batteries in it.

The problem was simple – the batteries were flat and needed topping up.

I told the main guy that I had to go and get some parts but should be able to help. I also said that I had to carry out the repair unwatched which amazingly he agreed to. I went back to our Embassy, organised some distilled water and reported the situation to the MI6 guy.

On return I was taken back into the Strong Room where incredibly they shut the door behind me. I topped up the batteries and in no time at all the kit sparked into life. Unfortunately being mechanical it made loud enough noises that they knew immediately when it was up and running again so I didn't get to see any of the information that came through.

I did however have plenty of time to get the other intel MI6 needed.

That evening the team went out for a few drinks at a local bar famous for its bottled beer menu that listed over 200 beers.

I had my friend R staying (yes the same one that I nearly ended my career with at a Millwall game) and we started ordering weird and wonderful beers from the menu. I remember there being a beer called 'Nude beer' and we both looked at the waitress and thought it was a 'must order' just in case!

Sadly it was an obscure Spanish beer that had a girl on the label with a scratch off bikini. Still it kept our simple minds busy for a few minutes.

A few pepper, cherry and god knows what else beers later the whole team were pretty merry and starting to relax – a little too much.

Two of the guys had become totally oblivious to the fact that we had guests amongst us and started to discuss the day's events at the other Embassy in earshot of R. I watched his ears prick up like an alerted Alsatian which is when I realised too much was being said. It was too late however and whilst R had a big grin on his face, the two guys were mortified. I don't think I've ever seen anyone sober up so quickly. Lucky for them, what happens in nude beer bar stays in nude beer bar and other than a bit of piss taking, no more was said.

QUEEN AND COUNTRY

EIGHTEEN

THE US YEARS 1988 – 1990
DI

Lisa Stansfield was at No 1 with 'All around the World', Indiana Jones was released at the cinema and the Berlin Wall had been ripped down after 30 years.

Princess Diana could do no wrong in the US. To them she was the acceptable face of a monarchy they didn't have and even better a real life princess. If Disney could do royalty she would be it.

The only other British woman held in such high regard, some would even say trumping Diana, was Mrs Thatcher.

We were all put on alert that Princess Di was visiting Washington to do a fund raising dinner for one of her charities and would be taking tea with the Ambassador in the afternoon. The cost to the American great and good to attend the dinner was £5000 a head and it had sold out straight away.

We knew what all of this meant. There would be teams of Police Royal Protection Branch all over the Embassy as well as Special Forces posted at appropriate locations.

Typically there would be an advance party to do a reccy of the area which was usually the first problem. Often in these situations people would get into 'clearance' wars about who could go into what areas and in reality these were no more than pissing competitions to see who would win.

The dinner was being held in a huge marquee set up for the occasion and surprisingly Lady Diana had only brought a few police officers with her as she thought it inappropriate to have high profile security during a charity dinner. To make matters worse for the police, on arrival she insisted that she would meet the families, particularly the children, of Embassy employees after her meeting with the Ambassador.

The plan was to invite all Employee families to gather in the Ambassadors garden and she would appear at one end walk along the path and then go back into the building at the other end.

The US Secret Service were going to provide a presence all around the perimeter of the Ambassador's residence but the Protection Branch wanted to take responsibility for letting people in and checking ID. That meant they needed extra bodies to organise the families inside the garden and keep the path clear which is where we came in.

We were invited to a security briefing the morning of the 'garden visit' as it was now known, Princess Di had asked that the children be brought to the front lining the path as she wanted to stop and talk to a few of them. A rope was going to be put up lining each side of the garden path and the four of us were to be stationed, one at the beginning one at the end and two in the middle somewhere, with the sole remit of keeping adults (especially pushy mums) back behind the rope.

Our other role was to show the Special Forces the roofs vantage points as the Ambassador's Residence was adjacent to the Embassy in Massachusetts Avenue and our team knew the buildings better than anyone.

On the day of the visit, the garden was rammed with people and we set about organising the kids at the front. As it happened, with two rows of kids sat down, the rest of the crowd were further back from the rope which made it easier to prevent encroachment. In the build up to her arrival there was an air of real excitement, and there was a huge cheer when she appeared. She stayed to form, walking up the path stopping regularly to crouch down and chat to one of the kids.

Me and the other guys were hamming it up a bit by talking bollocks into our walkie-talkies just to look important.

When she got to the end of the path, just about where I was standing she turned to the crowd and waved, again to a large cheer.

To my complete shock she then turned to me and shook my hand before going back into the residence.

After she'd gone the walkie-talkie jumped into life with the others calling me all the wankers under the sun.

In the next few days, just to really wind them up, it seemed that the official photographer was taking his final pictures at the moment she shook my hand and one of them was used in Embassy Communications regarding the visit.

There followed a good few weeks of piss taking at my expense.

FINN MAEDAN

QUEEN AND COUNTRY

NINETEEN

THE US YEARS 1988 – 1990
MAGGIE

New Kids on The Block were at No 1 with 'You Got It', Back to the Future 2 was released at the cinema and the Communist Party in Czechoslovakia stepped down to make way for democratic elections.

As mentioned earlier the one woman the Americans held in even higher esteem than Princess Di was Margaret Thatcher. They yanks love strong leaders, especially if they had a record of kicking ass at some point and if you asked any of them Mrs T took back the Falklands in 1983 by going down there and bashing up the Argies personally.

To many Americans Mrs T was the female version of the much loved Ronald Reagan who throughout the Cold War had stood firm against Gorbachev, often pushing him to the limit. He had brought the 'Star Wars' defence initiative to the table which although completely unpractical was exactly the sort of jingoistic fervour that the US loved. Perhaps the most poignant moment was the fall of the Berlin wall in 1989, something that many attribute, at least in part, to Reagan's doggedness.

Mrs Thatcher visited the US on numerous occasions in her time as Prime Minister but the visit that had the biggest impact on me was in 1989 when a special ceremony was being held on the White House lawn for her to say goodbye to a retiring Ronald Reagan. The two of them were the epitome of the 'special relationship' between the two countries and shared many political views and battles with the Eastern Bloc. Politics and world staging aside, the truth is they were genuinely friends.

Two of us were selected, myself and A to be responsible for Mrs Thatcher's communications during her visit. The US government had assigned her Blair House (spot the irony) for the duration of her visit mainly because it was in close proximity to the White House but also due to the fact it was an elegant and historic building, something there aren't too many of in Washington DC. Her communication team arrived the day before and we worked with them to set everything up in a Victorian style drawing room in Blair House.

It wasn't the most convenient of places to do this as there was hardly any power sockets and only basic air conditioning but we were used to 'making do' as were her team. We had a few tables brought in and set everything up from teleprinters and cypher gear to radio and satellite communications and even 'the button' (the capability to launch a nuclear missile from a briefcase) that followed her everywhere.

The day of her arrival me and A were hanging around in the war room as we affectionately called it when she walked in with her personal aide. She asked who we were and then thanked us for our help. Just as she was leaving her aide turned to me and said;

'Mr's Thatcher has asked if you would remove that book from the bookshelf. Thank you'

'What book?'

'The red one – 'History of the Labour Party''.

I went over to an ornate glass fronted bookcase that was against the far wall and found the book she described. I had heard Mrs T was a stickler for detail but how on earth she spotted that book I will never know.

A few minutes later there was a slight commotion in the door way. One of MRs T's team called me over and said;

'The miserable old bastard wants to speak

to someone from the Embassy – good luck.'

Dennis Thatcher was standing there with an angry look on his face.

'Get me todays Times boy. Stop whatever you are doing and go and get it now.'

I was a little taken aback. He was after all the Prime Ministers husband but at 25 I regarded myself as getting on rather than a 'boy' and in any case there were two problems, one I was under instruction not to leave the room and two, we only got papers a day late at the Embassy. Luckily his assistant had ushered him away and then returned to say;

'Forget about the paper, he's just grumpy because he didn't finish the crossword. I'll sort him out'

We were finalising some tests on the communication equipment when one of Mrs T's team said the Secret Service were outside the room and needed to speak to us. As friendly as we were with the yanks, we couldn't let them into that room so all went into the corridor. A typical clean cut, dark blue suited agent handed us all a small lapel badge.

'These are your assigned badges. Wear them at all times and note they will expire after the White House ceremony tomorrow.' With that he left.

The badge was just a navy blue square with a white circle in it, a bit boring but would make a decent keepsake of the occasion. I put mine in my pocket ready to put on my jacket lapel later. I went back into the room to speak to A when another of Mr's T's guys said.

'Where's your badge?'

'In my pocket. I'm going to put it on my jacket.'

'I'd get it on now mate. He wasn't joking when he said wear it at all times and don't make the rookie mistake of taking your jacket off with the badge attached.'

'What's the big deal?'

'Come with me.' He walked me to the curtains.

'Look out there at the roof opposite' There were snipers positioned at various locations.

'They're just the ones you can see. If the shit hits the fan at any point, anyone not wearing a badge goes down first.'

I never took that badge off again.

QUEEN AND COUNTRY

TWENTY

The Park
END GAME

In 1989, the first computers were installed in the unclassified area of the British Embassy in Washington DC. Yes, the government was years behind business where computers were becoming the norm and yes these beasts were 286's, stand alone, shrouded in copper to stop them radiating information and could only share data via 5.25 inch floppy disks, but for me it was a sign.

It was one of those quirky twists of fate that this seemingly innocuous event coincided with the world changing news that the Berlin Wall coming down but the two events were symbolic of how OSD was about to change forever.

The Berlin Wall coming down was not only the end of communist rule in East Germany but marked the beginning of the end of the Eastern Bloc or Iron Curtain. The Cold War was coming to an end and enemies were desperate to become friends.

Computers, and all other forms of Information Technology were starting to transform the workplace as well as how people communicate. There was no email outside of a few university laboratories and Tim Berners Lee was preparing to publish the first internet webpage a year later but a technical revolution had started.

The computers we installed in DC were IBM at their core but had been 'modified' for government use. As a consequence me and the other OSD guys on post were sent been on a special training course at the National Security Agency (NSA) the US equivalent of GCHQ. It was on that course I decided I liked the idea of working with computers, everything seemed to be based on logic and seemed to just make sense. I decided to take things further and signed up for a series of night school classes starting with DOS the basic computer operating system before going on to study database and spread sheet theory. IT as it was starting to be called was almost the only thing I had worked on in 10 years that had any value or demand outside of The Park.

Having returned from Washington I was assigned to a new section where short trips again loomed. The world was changing at a pace and as more and more communist regimes fell it was starting to become confusing as to who the enemy were.

One thing was certain, OSD needed to adapt and fast. We started to notice the list of short trips getting smaller which was closely followed by overseas positions being cut. The knock on effect of both being that more and more blokes were back in the sections scrapping over fewer and fewer trips. Meanwhile technology was in danger of completely passing everyone by. As the months went on, budgets were cut further. We all knew OSD had to change but is seemed cuts were preferred to re-purposing and at a time when neither 9/11 or 7/7 could even be imagined it was becoming harder for government to justify OSD's role.

I thought that the little IT skills I had obtained may be just enough to blag my way into a real world job and somehow I managed it.

That was the end of my 14 years with OSD. The Cold War was over, and with new technology and a new world order those days would never return. It was time to move on.

So that's about it. If you've got this far it's either because you've found this an interesting account of a time that has gone by or you've just woken up with dribble down your chin having fallen asleep at the first chapter and now you're skipping to the end. Either way, I've achieved what I set out to do, leave my memories for my children to enjoy or fall asleep to.

If you know me, none of what I have written will excuse my numerous character flaws but some of it may help explain some of them. Like most little boys who had an Action Man I dreamed of being a soldier one day and though I was never in the armed forces, we fought our own battles in the Cold War.

All in all, I like to think that I, Finn Maedan, did my little bit for queen and country

FINN MAEDAN

40894349R00102

Made in the USA
Middletown, DE
26 February 2017